THE UNDERSTUDY

JACK WEYLAND

THE UNDERSTUDY

A NOVEL

Deseret Book

Salt Lake City, Utah

No part of this book may be reproduced in any
form or by any means without permission in writing
from the publisher, Deseret Book Company,
P.O. Box 30178, Salt Lake City, Utah 84130

First printing March 1985
Second printing November 1985

Library of Congress Cataloging-in-Publication Data

Weyland, Jack, 1940-
    The understudy.

    I. Title.
PS3573.E99U5 1985   813'.54   85-1468
ISBN 0-87747-673-X

CHAPTER ONE

A cabin in the woods is good for a boy growing up, but sometimes he doesn't realize it until later in life.

The cabin from my boyhood sits in northwestern Montana, the last cabin on the dirt road that runs past Grizzly Gulch Lake. It sits on a hill, partially hidden by pine trees, but from the front steps you can see the clear blue water of the lake. It was made from lumber taken from a condemned building torn down when I was about six years old. My dad and a friend of his bid on the job and got it. Every night after work they removed boards and threw them in the pickup. They even tried to save the nails, but most of them came out bent.

With that lumber and the money they earned from demolishing the building, they put up two cabins by the lake. Ours was the second one built. By then they were running out of materials, so it ended up a hodgepodge of mismatched, odd-shaped, and warped boards. As a boy it was easy for me to imagine, especially during thunderstorms, that instead of being built, our cabin had been conjured by the spell of a demented witch.

Dad tried to get me to help with the cabin, but after a few minutes I'd get bored and complain until finally he'd let me run off to play. My favorite activity then was catching frogs to terrify my older sister, Beth.

That all seems so long ago now.

The cabin has always been there for us, in the good times and even in the bad.

*   *   *   *   *

Three summers ago, when the doctor released my father from the hospital, it was to send him home to die. The cancer was widespread, and there wasn't much that could be done.

1

I flew in from Los Angeles a week after Dad had been sent home. My sister, Beth, met me at the Kalispell airport. As soon as I saw her, I could tell she was still mad because I hadn't come right after she'd called to tell me he was failing fast.

"Hello, Beth," I said as I entered the terminal building.

"Hello, Michael," she said curtly. "How nice you could come."

Unless you know her, you might not realize that "How nice you could come" was her version of a slap in the face.

"Beth, I couldn't just walk out. I had to finish the movie I was doing."

"Of course," she said with an angry toss of her head. "We can't all be Hollywood stars, now can we?"

I sighed. "I'm not a Hollywood star. I'm just an actor who needs the work."

"Yes, and that's all you'll ever be, too."

I had a carry-on bag so we didn't have to wait for luggage. We walked outside.

"Pamela didn't come?" she asked.

"This is finals week at USC. She has exams. She'll come later."

"I would certainly hope so," she replied sullenly.

A few minutes later we were in Beth's pickup, driving home.

"How's Dad?" I finally asked.

"Why don't you tell me how you think he is?"

"All right, Beth, lay off. I know how he is."

"Well, you don't act like it. I've had to carry everything on my shoulders while you've wasted your time being an actor. What kind of a job is that, pretending you're somebody else? You think I don't dream of being somebody else? Sure I do. Lots of times. It's no picnic around here, I'll tell you. But at least I stick to what needs to be done. I'm not like you, Michael. We can't depend on you for anything when it comes to this family. It's always up to good old Beth. Well, I'm sick and tired of it."

"I know it's been hard on you, what with Dad and Wally." Wally was her husband.

She had tears in her eyes, but we didn't say anything about it. In our family we never did.

A minute later she said bitterly, "Dad keeps asking for you." She shook her head. "It's not fair. I do all the work, and he asks for you."

I thought about hugging her, but it would have been awkward. We've never hugged much in our family, and at a stoplight in a '62 Chevy pickup with a tricky clutch is probably not the place to begin.

"Do you want to see Wally?" she asked.

"Sure, Beth."

"Might as well. We need some gas anyway."

We pulled into Gas for Less, a run-down station on the edge of town. We both got out to run the self-service pump. "I can do it," she said. "You go talk to Wally."

When I got to the office, I saw a hand-scrawled note on the door that read "Out for lunch. Be right back."

I turned around. Beth was standing there, her head bowed, her hand to her face. "The pump's turned off," she said, sounding like it was the end of the world.

"There's a note that says he's out for lunch."

She sighed. "We both know where he is."

She drove us to the Stockade Bar.

The place had been built a long time ago, when people could still afford wood. The long mahogany bar was solid and dark and smelled of stale beer. A pool table sat in the middle of the room. On a wooden plank on the wall were all the local livestock brands. There was a dart board on another wall, and a wagon wheel with a clock in its center. And behind the bar, whiskey bottles were arranged in neat, orderly rows.

Wally was the only customer. He was sitting at the bar watching a British-Norwegian soccer game on a satellite sports channel. As soon as he saw Beth, he tossed his money down. "Well, gotta be going now, Frank," he said to the bartender. "Time to get back to work, you know."

"Yeah, well, don't work too hard," the bartender said.

Wally saw me in the doorway. "Well, well, look who's here!" he said with a wide grin. "Hey, Michael, how's it going?"

"Fine, Wally. How're things with you?" We shook hands and stepped outside.

"Can't complain. Of course, wouldn't do any good if I did, right?"

We chuckled. "Right," I said.

Beth exploded. "Wally, you said you'd quit leaving the station unattended anymore."

"Well, gosh, can't a man even have a little lunch around here?"

"I packed you a lunch," she grumbled.

He acted surprised. "You did?"

"Don't give me that! You know I did. You were just looking for an excuse to go drink."

"One beer is all I had. Look, ask the bartender if you don't believe me."

"When have you ever given me a reason to believe anything you say? And how can you sit there drinking all afternoon when we don't even have enough food to put on the table to feed our kids? And what are they supposed to do about school clothes in the fall?"

"Oh, I don't know," he muttered. "You always figure out something."

"If you were a real man, you'd take care of your family and not leave it up to me. I have no respect for a man who won't provide for his family." With a quick glance, she also tossed that barb in my direction.

A man can take only so much. "All right, you can stop now. I'm going back to work." Wally jumped in his pickup and roared away.

Beth drove us home.

When we pulled up, Mom came out to greet me.

It's hard to describe my mother the way she is now. But I can tell how it was when I was growing up.

We had a garden every year. She made me help with it. I hated string beans the worst. They just kept producing until I hated to look at another bean.

In high school she waited up for me after every date, and asked the same question night after night, "Did you treat your date with respect?"

I never saw my parents kiss each other, although I assume they must have once in a while. Ours was a no-nonsense household with chores to be done. As I grew up, I came to cringe whenever Mom called out, "Michael, what are you doing?" There would be a long pause, and finally I'd answer, "Watching TV." And she'd say, "Get in here and help out."

Mom had one weakness though. She liked to read paperback romances. In contrast, I never saw my father read anything but the newspaper. I think Mom could relate to my interest in fantasy. She shamed my father into going to all the high school plays I was in. And after graduation, she was the only one in our family who didn't discourage me from becoming an actor.

Shortly after graduation, when I went to California to seek fame and fortune as a Hollywood star, she bragged to the neighbors about every little part I got. But as the months dragged by, it must have finally dawned on her that the great success we'd hoped for wasn't going to be. As time went on, the scrapbook she'd kept for me since grade school required fewer and fewer entries.

Mom centered her life around her family. I've never asked if it was worth it, maybe because I'm afraid of the answer.

That day when I saw her, she looked very tired. We hugged. "Pamela and Jimmy didn't come with you?" she asked as we continued up the walk. My son Jimmy was nine years old.

"Pamela has final exams. She'll come later."

"And how's Jimmy?"

"He's fine, Mom."

"I thought at least he'd be coming with you."

"No, Mom. He'll come later with Pamela."

Beth couldn't leave it alone. "I can't believe the real reason she didn't come was because of exams. Wouldn't a teacher excuse her if she told him that her father-in-law was dying?"

"You just won't lay off, will you. All right, the real reason she didn't come is that she knows she'll have to come for the funeral anyway, and she doesn't want to make two trips in such a short time. She says we can't afford it."

Beth grumbled under her breath.

Mom and I continued up the walk. "We haven't told your father anything about what he has" Mom explained. "We think it's better this way."

In our family we'd quit saying the word *cancer*.

"Okay."

We continued inside. Mom went with me into the bedroom. It was dimly lit and smelled of pain. The bedstand groaned with glasses and bottles of pills.

"Dale," she said quietly, "Michael's here."

He opened his eyes and looked up at me.

"Leave us alone," he said to Mom. She left.

"Can I open the shades and let some light in?" I asked.

"I don't care. Do whatever you want."

I opened the curtains and turned around to see my father bathed in sunlight. His face was gaunt, and his strength was gone.

"Did Pamela or Jimmy come with you?"

"No, they'll come later."

"You mean for the funeral? What good is that going to do me?"

I smiled optimistically. "What are you talking about? You'll be up in no time."

"Have I ever lied to you?" he asked.

"No."

"Then don't lie to me. I'm dying, aren't I?"

I felt my throat clamp shut.

I tried stumbling again through "being up in no time."

"Don't give me that. Tell me the truth. Am I dying?"

It took a while, but finally I answered him. "Yes, Dad, you are."

He sighed. "That's what I thought."

When I returned to the living room, Beth, who'd listened in through the partially open door, was furious that I'd told Dad the truth.

Over the next few days, my father somehow willed himself to get strong enough to make all the necessary preparations. He called in a lawyer and made out his will, gathered all the insurance forms together, and picked a reasonably priced casket and burial site.

Then he lay back and waited to die.

But death, like sleep, does not always come when invited. He even seemed to improve a little.

One warm June day, he looked out his window and said, "I want to go up to the lake."

Of course, it was impossible. That's what my mother said. That's what Beth and Wally said.

But the doctor didn't agree. "If he feels up to it and somebody goes along and does most of the work, why not?"

"Well, I'm not taking him up there," Beth said. "He needs to be in town so that if an emergency happens, we'll be able to get him to the hospital."

"At this point I don't see what difference it makes," I said.

Beth glared at me.

And so I volunteered to take Dad for one last trip to our cabin. After a flurry of planning and buying groceries and stocking up on pills and going through my mother's long and detailed instructions of how to care for him, one morning I dropped the last box in the back of Dad's pickup and returned to the living room for him. He sat on the couch, still exhausted just from the effort of getting dressed.

I helped him down the front stairs. A minute later I had him inside the pickup. I closed the door and went in to get his sunglasses.

Beth confronted me in the living room. "I just want you to know that I think it's a terrible mistake for him to go traipsing off like this," she said.

"Beth, he doesn't love me more than he does you. It's just that I'm his son."

She went into the bathroom and locked the door. I could hear her crying even though she kept running water in the basin so we wouldn't know.

As I drove up the canyon, Dad looked out the window at the twisting mountain stream running alongside the road.

"I'd forgotten how nice it is up here," he said, looking

strangely out of place in his old, but now much too large, sweater that Mom had insisted he wear.

This is his last trip up here, I thought.

He pointed out the window. "See there, where the river goes under that railroad bridge? Right there on that point of land is a good place to fish. The water's fast, so you'll need about eight split-shot weights maybe two feet from the hook. Try it and you'll always get two or three nice trout."

"You always make it sound easy."

"Well, I've spent the past twenty years fishing around here. I've learned things that nobody else knows. I should write it all down. Somebody ought to benefit from all I know about this river."

We drove in silence for several miles while Dad studied each fishing hole.

I never did like fishing. When I was little, I was always scolded for throwing rocks in the water. And even after I got older, it got worse. To Dad fishing was a religion, and to not keep your rod up while reeling in was a sin.

The last time I went fishing with Dad was when I was thirteen. After that I was always able to find an excuse.

As we drove, he continued to fill me in on the fishing strategy for the best places on the river. None of it was of much interest to me.

We're strangers, I thought, as we continued up the canyon.

After we arrived at the cabin, I made several trips back and forth from the pickup with our supplies. Then we ate the lunch that Mom and Beth had prepared for us.

After lunch he took his pills and lay down for a nap. Three hours later he woke up and said he felt good enough to go fishing.

I carried two lawn chairs down to the lake, and then the fishing equipment, and after that a sunshade Mom had made me promise I'd set up for Dad. After everything was set up, I helped him down the trail to the lake.

I cast out and handed him the rod to hold, and then I sat down and waited. A short time later the bobber dipped.

"Gotcha," he said, setting the hook.

He reeled in and I netted the fish. Then, at his request, I released it again back into the lake.

A short time later he caught another.

A father and his son who were fishing nearby came over and asked what Dad's secret was. Dad gave them the complete history of fishing on the lake for the past twenty years.

The longer he fished, the more optimistic he became.

"This is just great," he said.

"I'm glad you're having a good time."

"Are you sure you don't want to fish?" he asked.

"No, I'm enjoying watching you. How are you feeling?"

"I haven't felt this good in months."

I cast out again for him.

"I've been thinking," he said, "how'd you like to go to Mexico with me for a few weeks? There's a hospital there where they treat people with diseases like mine. They say they can cure people even worse off than me."

I knew about private sanitoriums in Mexico where the very rich went in desperation, hoping for a miracle cure. They often died there.

He continued. "We don't have to just sit around and accept things, do we? We can fight back. We'll leave next week, just you and me. And when I'm all cured, then we'll have Mom and Beth fly down and we'll show them Mexico. Maybe we'll even take a boat through the Panama Canal. How does that sound?"

"Sure, Dad, whatever you say."

He kept talking about getting well and the whole family taking a boat through the Panama Canal, and how we'd stand at the railing and look out and maybe we'd even see wild animals in the jungle.

An hour later he was tired. I made the several trips necessary to get him and our baggage back to the cabin.

Just before we ate supper, he took his pills.

After supper, dark clouds rolled in, and by dusk we were in the middle of a storm. Looking out the window, I watched the wind drive sheets of rain across the lake in sporadic patterns. Lightning lit up the sky around us.

Suddenly Dad looked very sick. His forehead was dotted with

perspiration. He slowly got into his pajamas and took his arsenal of pills and crawled into the metal cot we used for beds in the cabin.

I stayed up and read an old Zane Grey paperback I'd found in the cabin. It was about a man who, whenever things got tough, saddled up his horse and headed into the wilderness. I wondered what happened when he ran out of wilderness.

At ten-thirty, I went to bed.

At midnight Dad woke up gagging. He vomited his supper.

I turned on the light. He was sitting up, his feet on the floor, his body hunched over with pain.

I got a pan of water and a towel and began to clean up the mess on the floor.

"I'm sorry," he said. "It must've been the pills."

"Don't worry about it. It's no problem."

I wiped up the floor and then cleaned him up as best as I could. I got him out of his pajamas and into a pair of old pants and a shirt. He was afraid to take any more pills because he might throw up again. So he sat on the edge of the bed and rocked back and forth, his head down, his teeth clenched, fighting against his invisible enemy.

Finally, at one-thirty, with the pain unbearable, he asked for a slice of bread, a glass of water, and his pills.

I helped him with his pills and then turned off the light.

The night was still being besieged with ragged flashes of lightning and the crash of thunder.

"Forget what I said about Mexico," Dad said in the darkness.

I ached for him. Mexico, his last hope for survival, had just slipped away in the harsh reality of that night.

"Besides, who wants to see the Panama Canal anyway?" he said. "You probably can't see any jungle animals from the boats."

There was a long agonizing silence and then he said, "You know, except for the movies, I've never seen lions running free."

Like a school of teasing dolphins, his boyhood dreams were

surfacing one last time before they slipped forever beneath a dull gray sea.

I wondered how old he'd been when he first dreamed about seeing lions running free? All the years I'd known him he'd never mentioned it, all the time we'd spent together fixing things around the house, taking care of things—while time rushed by without my ever knowing that my dad used to dream about seeing lions running free.

Now it was too late for lions.

*   *   *   *   *

The next morning was overcast and the rain continued in a steady drizzle.

Dad was barely able to get out of bed. He asked if we could go home.

A while later when we got in the pickup to leave, he said, "I want you to have the cabin when I'm gone. If I give it to Beth, she'll just sell it. I want it to stay in the family."

I nodded my head.

He slept most of the way back. The rocky rapids and deep holes of his river slipped past him for the last time as we made our way down the twisted mountain road.

Three weeks later he died.

CHAPTER TWO

His funeral was held at the First Methodist Church in Kalispell.

The minister was new to the area and had never even met my father. He knew my mother because she attended church once in a while. "I'm told that the deceased was a good husband and father and worked hard for his family. He was a devoted sportsman, and because of that, perhaps he didn't go to church as often, as he might have otherwise."

"Why is he saying that?" Beth complained to me.

Mary Ellen Ferguson sang. She has a singing voice that is only heard at funerals.

After the funeral we had a family lunch. Some of the food was brought by the women's auxiliary of the Elks Club that Dad belonged to. One of his best friends came to the lunch. He smoked a cigar. A few minutes later Pamela announced she had to go outside or she was going to be sick because of that wretched smell.

I went with her and told her it was rude to say that to one of dad's friends. She said it wasn't rude, it was just being self-assertive.

Jimmy was playing on a neighbor's swing set.

"Get him back here," she grumbled. "He has no business there."

I shrugged my shoulders. "He's not doing any harm."

"It's always up to me, isn't it?" she said. "You never discipline him. With you in the house, it's like having two boys instead of just one." She turned to Jimmy and yelled, "You get out of there before I take a stick to you! One! . . . Two! . . ."

The rules were that if you know what's good for you, never let your mother get to three.

Jimmy didn't budge. "Dad, do I have to?"

"No, it's okay. You can stay there."

She turned and glared at me.

"Pamela, let it be. He's okay. The neighbors don't mind."

"I've got to get out of here. I'm taking a walk."

"I'll go with you."

We started walking. "Mom was wondering how long you'll be staying," I said.

"I'm going back tomorrow."

"What for? I thought you were all through with classes."

She hesitated. "Michael, I've been accepted to medical school, and I need to make arrangements for the fall."

"When did this happen? I didn't know you'd even applied to med school."

"You knew I was majoring in pre-med, didn't you? Well after pre-med comes med."

"But I thought you were just taking classes for fun. You're not really serious about all this, are you?"

"I'm not surprised you don't know about my plans. You've never known anything that happens in this family. I nearly had to send you a birth announcement when Jimmy was born."

Every time we argued she brought it up. The day Jimmy was born, I was on location in a secluded area doing a film. A few days later when I got back in town, she was already home from the hospital. She never forgave me for not being there.

"What med school are you going to?" I asked.

She paused. "It's in Boston."

My mouth dropped open. "Boston? How can you go to med school in Boston when we live in L.A?"

She stopped walking. "Michael, I know this isn't a good time for you. And I wasn't going to bring it up until we got back home, but I might as well tell you now that I've decided to get a divorce. The papers are already prepared. If I thought about it, I could've brought 'em up with me on the plane and saved postage."

I was stunned. "You want a divorce? Why?"

"Don't take it personally. It's just that I want a career. Is that asking too much? Look, if you're worried about losing Jimmy, don't be. Because I'm giving him to you. I had him the first nine years of his life while you ran around pursuing what we laughingly called an acting career. So now it's my turn. You can have him the next nine years. I've decided that what I really want out of life is to become a gynecologist.''

"A divorce? There must be med schools in California. Can't we work something out?''

"Boston is very highly rated. I'd be foolish to turn it down. I leave next week. I brought all of Jimmy's clothes with me, in case you want to stay up here for a while. Also, I assume you'll want me to have the car and the stereo because I paid for them with the money I earned.''

"I can't believe this!'' I yelled. "You're divorcing me because Boston is highly rated? That doesn't make sense.''

"No, there's a lot more. I wasn't going to say it, but the truth is, I can't stand to live with you anymore.''

"Why not?''

"Some months you work and we have enough to get by, but then weeks pass with you sitting home all day watching TV soaps and yelling at the actors, 'I can do better than that!' You know the thing that really gets me? There's no guarantee that it'd ever be any different. I look ten years down the line, and I see us living in the same crummy apartment. And another thing— I've raised Jimmy nearly singlehanded. All you've ever done is, once in a while, go outside and throw a ball with him. Everything else is up to me. Maybe if we'd shared responsibilities more—maybe if you'd had a regular job and we could've depended on a steady income—maybe if you'd have looked at me like a partner instead of your slave—maybe then the marriage would've worked. But it's too late now. Besides, I've changed. When we got married, I was just out of high school. I depended on you for everything, but now I'm older. And going to college has shown me that I've got a good mind. I just can't stand to let it go to seed. I've thought about it quite a bit, and I really think this is the best way for both of us.''

She ended it by telling me she thought it best under the cir-

cumstances that we didn't sleep in the same house that night.
She said she'd already made arrangements to stay at Beth's.

Later Beth told me the two of them stayed up very late that
night talking, no doubt trading off stories about how rotten their
husbands were. She said she admired Pamela for being able to
realize she'd made a mistake in her marriage, and then moving
on with the rest of her life. She said she hoped to be able to do
that someday too.

The next day Beth drove Pamela to the airport. When she
came back, she said she wanted to make one thing clear. I'm
sure it was something Pamela had warned her about. "Don't go
thinking that I'm going to baby-sit your kid while you run back
to Hollywood. He's your responsibility now, and it's time you
grow up and face it. So what are you going to do? Get a job?"

"No, I guess I'll go back up to the cabin."

"What about Jimmy?"

"I'll take him with me."

"I think we should sell the cabin—not that it's worth that
much. But there is the land. I had a real estate man look at it
recently, and he said he thought we could probably get forty
thousand for it. We could give Mom half and then split the other
half between us."

"I don't want to sell it."

"Why not? You never liked it up there anyway. If I had that
money, I could start going to college. Pamela said it'd be good
for me."

"We're not selling the cabin, Beth, so just forget it."

That made her mad. "Don't Mom and I even have a say in
this?"

"Dad gave the cabin to me."

"When did he do that?"

"When we were up there."

"I'm not saying I believe you, but even if he did, it was probably because he was delirious."

"You and Wally can use it anytime you want, but we're not
selling it. It'll always be in our family."

"You want to know something? I think Pamela's doing the

right thing in divorcing you. She deserves better than you. Anybody deserves better than you.''

Two days later I had Wally drive Jimmy and me up to the cabin.

*　　*　　*　　*　　*

It was a difficult time for me, trying to cope with losing a father and a wife in one week, and, almost as bad, gaining a full-time son.

Fishing was perfect for the way I felt. If a man goes to a shopping mall and spends hours staring at the people shuffling by, sooner or later he'll be suspected of either being a deviate or a bum. But take the same man and put him on the shore of a lake with a fishing pole in his hand, and he can sit there for weeks, never speaking to anyone, not shaving or washing or even eating much—and the entire world will look upon him as an outstanding person, a friend of nature.

Of course, actually catching a fish would have ruined everything, because then we'd have to worry about what to do with it—cleaning, filleting, frying, and then telling ourselves how good it tasted.

What I needed was some time to think, to try and sort out my life. It was as if, with Dad alive, there was a cushion of one generation to protect me from my own mortality. But with him gone, I was the next to go.

My father worked all his life as a surveyor for the state highway department. And yet who in the highway department would remember him in ten years?

Days slipped by while I wrestled with the parade of whys that marched through my mind.

One night I dreamed I was at the cabin and Dad walked up to me and said, ''I've seen the lions running free.'' I looked around and saw hundreds of jungle animals around him, and in particular, a large lion lying on the cabin porch. Dad walked up and scratched it behind the ears.

I woke up and spent the rest of the night wondering what it could mean.

He was a good father. When I got to be about ten years old, he began teaching me the things that were important to him. He'd say, "The car needs work. I need you to help me." So I'd go out to the garage with him. "Hold the light," he'd say, and that'd keep me there until he finished.

He never talked much while he worked, but once in a while he'd shake his head and say, "That's what I thought."

"What?"

"See there. That's the problem. Hold the light closer and let's see if we can get to it."

We fixed cars and did plumbing and house wiring and helped neighbors with carpentry, and once we even learned upholstery when we couldn't afford a new couch.

In some ways I didn't mind the time it took me away from my school friends. It was nice to know that out of all the men in town he could get to help, my dad wanted me.

The only time I ever saw him lose his temper was one time when I was fifteen and Mom was on me for something, and I sassed her back. He came over and jerked me out of the chair and said, "Don't you ever let me hear you talking like that to your mother again!"

He never understood why I wanted to be an actor. "Why waste your time when you could do something useful with your life? You've got the hands to become a carpenter or a plumber or a mechanic. Look, if you want, I'll even send you to college, and you can become an engineer."

"I know, Dad, but I want to be an actor."

He looked at me for a long time and then slowly shrugged his shoulders. "Well, I guess a man has to do what's in his heart."

When I left home, he and I stood there, watching the bus driver load my suitcase. Mom and I had already kissed each other goodbye. Beth had nodded goodbye to me.

I think Dad wanted to hug me. But he didn't. It just wasn't his style. Instead he stuck out his hand. "Whatever you do, do your best at it."

"I will, Dad." We shook hands awkwardly, and then I turned and eagerly jumped on the bus, believing that I was going off to a life of fame and fortune, and never for a moment considering what I was leaving behind.

I still love him very much.

He was my dad.

*   *   *   *   *

In addition to losing my father, I felt bad for having failed in my marriage. Where had I gone wrong with Pamela?

We'd married young. She was eighteen and I was eighteen and a half.

We met at a cut-rate acting school in Los Angeles. She was from Michigan. As a senior she'd been in a school play, playing Anne in *The Diary of Anne Frank*. Everyone in school said she could be a big star, and so after graduation she came to Hollywood to seek fame and fortune.

At any time in L.A. there must be hundreds of eighteen-year-old girls from all over the country who starred in their high school production of *The Diary of Anne Frank*. They come right after graduation, hoping to become famous. Instead they end up working at Jack-in-the-Box.

Just after I met her, I got a decent part in a movie. It paid good money. Thinking this was just the beginning of great success, I put a down payment on a new car and got a better apartment and asked Pamela to marry me.

Suddenly I was a grown-up person doing grown-up things—like marrying hastily and going into debt.

We were married by a justice of the peace. None of our family was there, mainly because we didn't tell them until it was done.

Just after we got married I tried out for a stage play. I wanted the lead, but I didn't get it. They gave me a small part and asked me to be the understudy for the lead role. And so every night I went on stage, gave my few lines, then spent the rest of the night offstage watching the lead actor until I knew by heart his every word and gesture.

I used to laughingly tell people that I was only a heartbeat away from being a big star.

One time the lead got stuck in traffic, and another time he went to the beach and fell asleep under the sun and got such a bad sunburn that he couldn't go on for two days, but mostly he was very healthy. And so my chance for instant stardom passed me by. The play ran three months, and then folded, and suddenly for the first time in California I was out of work.

To tide us over, Pamela got a job working at a dry cleaners and I scoured the city looking for bit parts. I did some TV ads. I became Grape Man for all the Fruit of the Loom commercials. It went very well, actually. I think I added a great deal to the role.

Then Pamela got pregnant, and eventually, because of morning sickness, she had to quit work.

Because we needed money to pay for the baby, I got a job working for the phone company, checking telephone poles to see if they were rotting away in the ground. We walked along rural phone lines. It was an easy job. I'd walk up to a pole, bury my hatchet into it, and shake it as hard as I could. If it broke, it was not a good pole.

A few months after Jimmy was born, Pamela's father sent her some money, and she started taking college courses.

At the lake I wondered if education was the thing that destroyed our marriage. I remember a reception we went to for honor students. Pamela didn't want me to go, but I insisted, since the invitation clearly said students and their parents or spouses.

We were standing in a crowd. A professor came up to us. "Pamela, who is this handsome guy with you?"

"Oh, he's my husband."

We shook hands. "What's your major?" he asked me.

"I'm not in college."

"Oh. What do you do?"

"I'm an actor."

"Is there anything you've done that I might have seen?"

"Well, do you watch TV?"

"Once in a while."

"Have you ever seen any Fruit of the Loom commercials? I'm Grape Man."

He turned to Pamela. "This is a joke, right?" he asked.

She shook her head.

He moved on to someone more promising.

That's why, when I heard about the Carl Sandburg part for a movie funded by the National Institute of Humanities, I tried out for the part and got it. It didn't pay all that much, but it was something you could tell a college professor without having him look at you like you were the village idiot.

It took Pamela several years, but finally she graduated.

*   *   *   *   *

"Dad?" Jimmy said to me one night just after we'd finished our supper of a can of pork and beans.

"What?"

"You never talk to me."

"I'm sorry. I've been thinking about a lot of things."

"Are you mad at me?"

"No. Why should I be mad at you?"

He looked away and barely whispered. "Because it was my fault that Mom got a divorce."

"It didn't have anything to do with you."

"I tried to keep my room clean and do my own clothes right there at the last, but I think she just got tired of me."

"That's not true, Jimmy. She loves you."

"Then why did she leave me?"

I sighed. "It was my fault, not yours. She left because I wasn't the kind of husband and father I should've been."

"Alan Cramer's father gets drunk all the time and beats up Alan's mother. You're better than that."

"Thanks."

"And Bobbie Elliott's dad ran off with his secretary. You never did that."

"No."

"Of course, you don't have a secretary."

"But even if I did, I'd never do a thing like that."

"So you're not that bad," he said.

I paused. "What are some of the things I could've done better as a dad?"

He paused, "You never came to my classroom and met my teachers."

"Anything else?"

"You were always gone. You missed my birthday last year."

"Anything else?"

"I wish you'd have made Mom happier, so she wouldn't have left us."

"Right," I said glumly.

"Dad, how many acting parts have you had?"

"Quite a few."

"What parts have you played?"

"Well, I was Grape Man . . . I was a police lieutenant in *Chainsaw Beach Party* . . . I was the poet Carl Sandburg in *Hog Butcher of the World* . . . I was an army officer in *Sunset over Saigon* . . ."

"But have you ever played the part of just a regular dad?"

A long pause. "No, I never have."

"I didn't think so."

That made me feel rotten.

"Did you have a good dad?" Jimmy asked.

"Yeah, he was real good."

"What was he like?"

We'd taken Jimmy to Montana a few times, but he was too young then to remember my parents.

"Dad was good at fixing things. We spent a lot of time working together. Did you know he built this cabin? The only time he left town was when he took us on a vacation. And whenever I was in anything at school, like a play or for a football game, he was always there with my mom."

"Dad, d'you think you could learn to be more like your dad?"

"I don't know. Maybe. I guess I can try."

We each got into our sleeping bags and lay down on our cots.

"You won't ever get tired of me and leave, will you?" he asked.

"Never."

"That's good, because I think I'm too young to get a job, aren't I?"

"Yeah, I think so."

*   *   *   *   *

I tried to be a better father, but it wasn't easy.

"How long are we going to stay here?" Jimmy asked as we sat and fished. It seemed like we'd been there forever, but it had only been two weeks.

"Just as long as you'd like," I said.

"Good, then let's leave today, because I don't like it up here."

"Some boys would think it was great to spend the summer at a cabin on the lake."

"I don't know why. There's nothing to do up here."

"What do you mean? We go fishing and take hikes, and in the afternoons we go swimming."

"Yeah, but there's no TV," he grumbled.

"It's not good to watch TV all the time."

"Also I don't like what we eat."

"What's wrong with what we eat?"

"All we have is pork and beans."

"That's not true. We have soup. We have bread. We have peanut butter and jelly. We have potatoes. And we have hamburger when I get a check in the mail."

"But there's no McDonald's or Burger King or video arcades or MTV."

"We don't need that. We're mountain men."

"Also, Dad, I think I should have milk to drink."

"What for? Coffee's cheaper. Besides, mountain men don't drink milk."

"But a boy my age needs calcium for his bones."

"What are you talking about? You've got as many bones as any kid who drinks milk. Anyway, who told you that about milk?"

"I read it in that Boy Scout manual I found in the cabin."

"I wish you'd throw that thing away," I grumbled. "It's caused nothing but trouble since we came here. We go on a hike and you spend all your time complaining that I'm leading you through poison ivy."

"But you were, Dad."

I frowned. "Well, yeah, but just that one time."

"You think we'll ever catch a fish?" he asked.

"Sure we will. Someday. You'll see."

"But how come everyone else catches fish except us?"

"Maybe there just aren't any fish where we happen to be fishing."

"But it doesn't matter where we go. We still never catch any."

"We will. You'll see."

"You·think Mom'll ever come back to us?"

"She might. Sure, why not?"

"I don't think she'd ever come to the lake though, do you?"

"No, I don't think so."

"So shouldn't we go back to California just in case she changes her mind about leaving us?"

"She'll contact us if she wants to come back."

He sighed. "How much longer do we have to fish today?"

"I'll tell you what. I've still got some money left. How about if we go to the general store on the other side of the lake and split a Fudgsicle?"

He shrugged his shoulders. "What's a Fudgsicle?"

"You don't know what a Fudgsicle is? It's like a Popsicle except I think maybe it's got some milk in it."

"I guess so."

We reeled in. He scowled at me. "Dad, you forgot to put worms on the hooks."

He was right. On purpose I hadn't put any worms on the hooks.

"I was just testing you to see if you'd notice. Let this be a lesson to you, always put a worm on the hook."

"Oh, Dad," he moaned.

*   *   *   *   *

Within the month Mom moved to Arizona to live with her sister, who lived in a trailer park near Phoenix.

Beth came out once to see if we were still alive.

"Do you have to wear that awful beard?" she asked, scowling at me.

"Hey, we're mountain men, right, Jimmy?"

"Aunt Beth, can I please go back to town with you?"

I chuckled. "He's just kidding. He loves it out here. Yesterday he caught our first fish."

"Dad made me eat it," he complained.

"You caught it, so you had to eat it. That's our rule. Tell Aunt Beth how delicious it was."

"It was full of bones," Jimmy complained.

"Yeah, but tell her how I gave you a dime for every bone you found."

"You said you would, but you haven't given me anything yet."

I frowned at him. "I will. Just give me a few weeks until I get another check."

"Aunt Beth, do you make your kids drink coffee, or do you buy them milk for their bones even though it costs more money?"

"What's this?" she asked me. "You're not giving him milk to drink?"

"Don't listen to him. Yesterday I bought a package of powdered milk, but he won't drink it."

"It tastes like chalk."

"Look around. Do you see any cows anywhere?"

Beth turned to me. "How long are you two staying up here?"

"All summer."

"And then what?"

I shrugged my shoulders. "Maybe we'll stay here in the winter too."

Jimmy objected. "Dad, I have to go to school."

"I can teach you here."

"What grade is he going to be in?" Beth asked me.

I turned to Jimmy. "Tell Aunt Beth what grade you'll be in."

"Fourth grade."

"That's right," I said, faking it. Pamela always took care of details like remembering what grade Jimmy was in.

"Michael, are you ever going to get a job and be normal?" Beth asked.

"I don't know. It's cheap living here, and I still have some money coming in from the movies I've done."

"Not much money from that, I'll bet. How many people would go see a movie about a hog butcher?"

"Beth," I grumbled, "I've told you before. It wasn't about a hog butcher. It was about Carl Sandburg, the poet who wrote 'Hog Butcher of the World.' "

She shrugged her shoulders. "Hog butcher, poet—what difference does it make? I still wouldn't go see it."

"Look, we knew when we filmed it that it wasn't going to be another *Star Wars*."

"That's for sure. I've never even met anyone who's seen it."

"It was very big in Chicago."

"Why don't you settle down and get a job?"

"Like what?"

"You can work for Wally."

"You mean baby-sit him, don't you? Look, I know you mean well, but pumping gas just isn't right for me."

"That's your trouble—nothing's right for you."

"By the way, how's Wally doing these days?"

"About like you. I still think we should sell the cabin so I can get my divorce sooner."

"We'll never sell the cabin."

She angrily got up to leave.

"Aunt Beth, please take me home with you," Jimmy pleaded.

"No, not today."

"Tomorrow then?" he asked hopefully.

I played my ace card. "Jimmy, don't forget that tomorrow we're going to take a hike to Meadowlark Springs."

"Please, Aunt Beth," he pleaded. "I'll wash dishes for you and empty the garbage and make my own bed. I won't be any trouble."

Beth left. Jimmy pouted about it all day.

*   *   *   *   *

One night we roasted marshmallows in a campfire we'd made in front of the cabin.

"See all those stars?" I said. "It makes you think, doesn't it?"

"What about?"

"It makes you think there must be a God, doesn't it?"

"Is there, Dad?"

I paused. "I think so."

"Is God like us, or is he different?"

I cleared my throat. "Well, in some ways he's like us and in other ways he's, uh, different."

"You don't know very much about God, do you?"

"No, not much."

*   *   *   *   *

In mid-July we had another visitor. He wandered around the lake and eventually made his way to where we were fishing. He had gray hair and looked distinguished. "I'm looking for someone named Michael Hill."

"That's me."

We shook hands.

"I'm Ben Jansen with the Atlantis Group. We're an independent movie company headquartered in Utah. We saw your portrayal of Carl Sandburg, and we were very impressed with the depth and sensitivity you gave to the role. I came all the way from Utah to see if we could interest you in doing a film for us."

"We're interested," Jimmy said quickly.

I smiled. "He's just kidding. Actually we love it out here among nature."

We walked up the trail to the cabin.

"Jimmy, why don't you pour Mr. Jansen a cup of coffee?"

"No thanks," Mr. Jansen said.

"Well, how about some hot chocolate then?"

"That'd be fine."

"Well, then fix Mr. Jansen a cup of your famous hot chocolate."

Jimmy picked up a cup and examined it. "This cup's got some gunk stuck to the bottom."

"What kind of gunk?"

He held the cup up to the sunlight streaming in the window. "I'm not sure. It's either stuck-on noodles from yesterday or a glob of burnt beans from the day before."

"Aw, that won't hurt anything." Then I noticed Jansen's expression. "Hey, but just to be on the safe side, take the cup down to the lake and rinse it out." I turned to our guest. "The pump's broken now, so we use lake water."

Jimmy started out the door and then stopped. "Do you want me to go to where we cleaned our fish last night? I told you we shouldn't have thrown its guts into the water."

"Better go a few feet from there."

Jansen saw a way out. "I really hate to put you to any trouble. How about if I just pass on the hot chocolate."

"How about a graham cracker?" Jimmy said. "The mice get into most everything, but I think you're pretty safe with an unopened packet of graham crackers."

I'd had it with my son. "While you're at it, Jimmy, why don't you go through your list of one thousand ways to die in the forest." I turned to Ben Jansen. "One tiny mouse gets into a few scraps of food and the kid gets hyper. Ben, take a graham cracker." It almost sounded like an order.

Ben carefully selected a graham cracker and took a small bite and then turned to me. "We're not a big company, and we can't pay you what Universal Studios might, but I think you'll be interested in the role. We're doing a movie about the life of Christ, and we'd like you to play the lead."

"Dad, please take the job. I can't stand it up here anymore."

"Go check our lines and see if we've caught a fish yet."

He came back a minute later, panting hard from having run all the way down the trail and back again. "You haven't told him no yet, have you?"

I turned to Ben. "I'm afraid it's really out of the question," I said. "My father died a few weeks ago, and right after that my wife got a divorce and left me with Jimmy. I've been trying to work it out, but I'm just not sure when I'll be ready to work again."

"We saw you in the Sandburg film and decided you were the one we want for the role. We like the way you project on the screen. Strong but sensitive. Courageous but kind. Bold but caring."

"Dad, is he talking about you?"

"Go wash that cup like I told you," I ordered. "One . . . two . . ."

He went outside and swished the cup in some rainwater and hurried back in again.

"I can't go dragging my boy all the way to Israel. He needs stability in his life now."

"No, I don't," Jimmy butted in. "Just get me away from this place."

"Actually we'll be filming in Utah," Ben said. "Much of the same scenery exists there as can be found in Israel."

"You still don't understand. It's not like I have someone to watch him while I'm doing a movie."

"My cousin takes in children. I'm sure we can work something out. We'll be filming not too far from Orem. You'd see Jimmy every night. And we won't be filming on Sundays."

"I still say the answer's no."

He paused. "May I ask why?"

"Well, besides all the other reasons, I'm not a religious man. I don't know anything about Jesus."

"Did you know anything about Carl Sandburg before you played that role?"

"Well, no, but . . ."

"It's probably the best role in the world. I can't understand why you'd turn it down. I'll be directing the movie, and I've come a long way to find you."

"Dad, please."

I paused. "Well, maybe I'll think about it."

Ben took us to supper. He gave Jimmy five dollars' worth of quarters to play video games at the pizza place we ate at. That won him Jimmy's friendship for life.

He outlined some very good terms for me, so that beside the straight salary, I'd be getting a percentage of the profits from the movie. Also, he phoned his baby-sitting cousin in Utah and had me talk to her. Her name was Kellie. She sounded acceptable enough.

By the end of the evening, with Jimmy threatening to run away if we didn't leave, I agreed to do the movie.

CHAPTER THREE

A few days later Jimmy and I pulled into Orem, Utah. We were driving an old station wagon we'd bought in Montana. It was a piece of junk, but it was all we could afford. It looked like the winner in a rust contest. It had paneling along the side, the kind that looks like real wood but is really just strips of wallpaper. Whenever I wasn't looking, Jimmy was peeling it off the car. I tried to get mad at him but had to admit it was irresistible. It was like after a bad sunburn when you try to see how long a continuous piece of dead skin you can peel off at one time.

"Now this one's a real peach cake," the salesman kept saying when we first looked at it in the used-car lot.

Peach cake, my foot. After we left on our trip, I found that when we went over forty miles an hour, the radiator began to spout steam. We had the only car on the highway that could be mistaken for Moby Dick. In fact, from that time we began to call it Moby Dick.

It was a long trip. We had one blowout and a vapor lock climbing a mountain pass just outside of Butte. We had to stop every hour and put more water in the radiator.

The night before we entered Utah, we slept under the stars at a rest stop on I-15 near Pocatello. Jimmy kept going on all night about the number of people who were mugged each year at rest stops late at night.

The next day, after arriving in Orem, we rented a small house and bought some food, using some money Ben had advanced me. I called his cousin the baby-sitter, and she asked us to come by after all the kids had left. Anytime after six, she said.

At six-fifteen we pulled up to her house. The yard was fenced

in, with a swing set in the front yard, and a small hand-lettered
sign that read "Peppermint Pals Day Care Center."

We walked up the walk and rang the doorbell.

"Just a minute," a voice called out.

"There's still time to escape," I said to Jimmy.

"It'll be okay, Dad."

A young woman with reddish brown hair and freckles
opened the door. Looking at her, I could tell it had been a hard
day. She had dried glue stuck to her faded BYU T-shirt, and the
place smelled like old diapers.

"I'm Michael Hill. I talked to you on the phone."

"Oh yes, come in," she said, trying to rearrange her hair with
her hand.

She opened the screen door. "I'm Kellie Green. Excuse the
mess."

We carefully made our way up the toy-strewn steps to her
living room. Once inside she focused her attention on Jimmy.
"And what's your name?"

"Jim Hill."

"He goes by Jimmy."

"Dad, I've told you before. I don't like the name Jimmy. It's a
girl's name."

"You ever hear of Jimmy Stewart?" I countered.

"I don't care. From now on, call me Jim."

"Jim," Kellie said, "I'm glad to meet you."

"Do you have any video games here in your house?" Jim
asked.

"No."

He looked discouraged. "Well, do you have anybody my
age?"

"How old are you?"

"Nine."

"My son is seven."

"Where is he now?"

"He's taking a violin lesson."

Jimmy, or Jim as he preferred, scowled. "Why?"

"He likes playing the violin."

Jim shook his head. "Why?"

"We'll look someplace else," I told him.

He shrugged his shoulders. "This is all right. After the lake, I can stand anything."

I turned to Kellie "I'd like to look around, if that's all right."

"Of course."

We walked through the house. As far as I could tell, she'd taken low-grade junk and turned it into games and projects for kids. Jim drifted into the backyard to check things out.

Letting her give me the guided tour, I had a chance to study her features without being too obvious. She had avocado green eyes and wore little or no makeup. She'd sewn patches on the knees of her slacks, and that, along with her freckles, made her seem a little bit like a character from Huckleberry Finn.

We passed a storeroom. There were large bags labeled "Wheat" lying on the floor.

"Is anything wrong?" she asked.

"Well," I chuckled, "from here it looks like you've got bags of wheat in your house. So tell me, what's really in the bags?"

"Five hundred pounds of wheat." She looked at me. "You know why, don't you?"

I paused. "Uh, let's see. It's got something to do with your religion, right? Like, is it some kind of an offering to the gods?"

"No, it's for emergencies."

"Oh."

"Is something wrong?" she asked, noticing my confusion.

"Uh, well, I'm just trying to imagine what kind of emergency it'd be where a person would suddenly need five hundred pounds of wheat."

"You're not a member of the church, are you?" she asked.

"You mean, a Mormon? Oh no. Are you?"

"Yes."

"Oh." I paused. "Uh, if I decide to let my son stay here, ·
you're not going to try to brainwash him or anything like that, are you?"

"No, of course not."

"That's good. I just want him to be like me as far as religion goes."

"I understand. What religion are you?"

"Well, I don't actually belong to a church. I guess you could say I'm tolerant and open-minded."

"Would you ever like to learn more about the Mormon church?"

"No thanks."

We continued with the tour.

"Tell me, what does your husband think about you running a day-care center?"

"Didn't Ben tell you? My husband died a few months ago."

"Oh, I'm sorry."

"He left me with no insurance and a son with special needs. Having a child-care center seemed like the best way for me to have an income without leaving home. And what about you?" she asked.

"My wife divorced me in June."

"I see."

"Yeah, she just walked out on me. One day out of the blue she tells me she wants to be a gynecologist. So now she's in med school in Boston. Well, I hope she's happy, because she's going to have to live her whole life knowing she abandoned her family. Now it's up to me to carry on." I knew I was milking the situation for sympathy, but I couldn't stop myself.

"It must be difficult for you. Ben says you're doing a movie for him."

"Yes. It's about the life of Christ."

"That explains why you have a beard then."

"Well, actually I had it up at the lake."

"The lake?"

Jim was outside, so he couldn't bad-mouth me. "Yes, I've spent the last few weeks with my son camping at a lake in Montana."

"You know, there're so few fathers that ever take the time to be with their sons. I go fishing with my boy sometimes, but I'm sure it's not the same as with a father and his son."

"Yes, it was really, uh, special. I don't think either of us will ever forget our experience at the lake. I know I won't."

"What part are you going to play in Ben's movie?"

I cleared my throat. "Jesus."

"Looking at you, I can see why they'd want you to play him."

"You can? Why?"

"You have a gentleness in your face that I associate with him."

That caught me off guard. It made me want to be helpful. "What's your son's name?"

"Russel."

"Maybe sometime I can take him fishing with me and my son."

"I'm sure he'd appreciate that. He needs a man's influence."

The tour was over. I called out the back door for Jimmy to get in the car.

I lingered at her door. It was the first time I'd talked to a single woman since my divorce.

"How much do you want for watching Jimmy?" I asked.

"Eleven dollars a day—that's from seven in the morning to five at night. That includes lunch too."

"Let me pay you fifteen."

She paused. "Why would you want to do that?"

"I don't think you're charging enough."

"You don't have to do that."

"Please let me."

"All right. Thank you very much."

Jimmy was waiting for me at the car.

"She's sort of nice, isn't she," he said when I got in the car.

"Don't slouch, Jimmy."

"Jim," he corrected.

CHAPTER FOUR

The next morning I dropped Jim off at Kellie's and made my way to the Atlantis Group offices in Orem. Ben Jansen wasn't in his office so I waited for him to return. Fifteen minutes later he breezed in. He was a man who gave the impression of always doing important things, but I noticed he had a picture of his large family on the desk.

"Are you all settled in?" he asked.

I nodded. "I've rented a house, and I took my son to Kellie Green this morning, so I guess I'm ready to start work."

He showed me around the office and introduced me to the people who worked there. He explained that Atlantis Group did about five films a year and marketed them to theaters all over the country. Some of the films were sold to cable TV as movies, while others made it into theaters.

"Do you have a completed script for me?" I asked when we were through with the tour.

"Sure, let me get one for you." A minute later he returned with a copy of the script.

"I've got a meeting in a few minutes, but maybe we could just talk through the first part so you'll know where we're coming from."

"Sure."

He sat down at his desk. "Okay, let's start at the beginning. It's morning on the Sea of Galilee. Fishing boats slip quietly toward shore after a long night's work. Seagulls circle overhead looking for a free meal from the fishermen. The camera pans from the shore to the foothills. We see a man taking an early-morning walk. It's the spring of the year. Wildflowers carpet the hills surrounding the lake. The rising sun catches the brightly colored petals. The camera moves to a closeup of the man in the middle of a large field of wildflowers. We see that it's Jesus. He bends over and touches one of the petals and appears to be studying it. As he does so, the camera features one of the flowers in microscopic detail.

"We hear a voice from another existence. 'Let the earth bring forth grass, the herb yielding seed, and the fruit tree yielding fruit after his kind, upon the earth.' "

Ben looked up at me. "What we want here is to show that Jesus was the one given responsibility by God the Father to create this earth. The same sun that in the beginning Jesus commanded to give light now warms his back. He walks on land that he once commanded to be separated from the waters. The sun, the rain, the animals, the flowers and trees and grain—he made them all. And yet here he stands, the son of a mortal woman and an immortal father, picking a bouquet of wildflowers to take home to his mother."

Ben leaned back in his chair. "We've got to make this point, because if we don't, then what is he? A good teacher at best. But he's more than that. He's the Son of God come to earth to show us the way."

I had questions but decided to let it go for now. "Okay, what happens next?"

"The camera follows him as he walks back home. He stops to watch the shepherds, how the sheep from each flock know the voice of their shepherd. All this he'll use in his parables.

"He enters the village of Nazareth and walks down the winding streets, passing small dusty houses. Neighborhood children, seeing him come, eagerly run out to meet him. He kneels down and talks with them and gives each one a flower from his bouquet, and then he continues on his way.

"We see him entering his boyhood home. Next to the cottage is a carpenter's shop. We switch to an interior shot. It's a small, neatly kept household. His mother sits in the sunlight of an open window, doing last-minute touches on a robe she's made. Jesus gives her the flowers he's picked and kisses her.

"Next we see Jesus wearing the robe for the first time. Mary is kneeling to make adjustments on the hem. This is the robe he'll wear throughout his ministry. Mary fusses with the robe. Jesus, full of love, reaches out and touches her head. Mary looks up and suddenly realizes her son is about to leave.

" 'Will you go away now?' " she asks.

"Jesus nods his head. Suddenly she becomes every mother just before her son is about to leave home. Where will he sleep? What will he eat? She promises to prepare his favorite food if he'll stay just a little longer.

"He smiles, shakes his head, and tenderly reminds her he must be about his Father's business.

"Next we see him leaving behind his boyhood home. Things will never be the same again for him or for his mother or for the entire world."

He paused. "I guess I don't have to tell you that the whole movie depends on your portrayal of the Savior."

A few minutes later he had to run off to a meeting. I drove to a park and sat on a picnic table and spent the day reading the script.

*   *   *   *   *

Around six o'clock I went to pick up Jim.

Kellie met me at the door looking frazzled and depressed. "I don't think I can have anybody come tomorrow."

"Why not?"

"The toilet backed up, and I had to send kids over to a neighbor's house all day to use the bathroom, and she just called to tell me that she's definitely not going to be home tomorrow." She had tears in her eyes. "A plumber's going to cost me a fortune."

"Let me look at it, okay?" I said.

After a brief inspection, I said to her, "I know just the thing to fix it. I'll be right back."

A few minutes later I returned from a hardware store with a toilet auger for fishing back through the pipes. In a few minutes I retrieved a diaper that somebody'd flushed down the toilet.

"Where did you learn to do that?"

"My dad taught me a lot of things." I paused. "He died this summer."

"I'm sorry. You really have had a rough summer, haven't you."

I nodded. "I'll leave this here so you can use it the next time it happens."

"How much do I owe you?" she asked.

"Nothing."

"Are you sure?"

"Positive."

"Well, at least stay for supper. It might take a while because I forgot to take the meat out of the freezer, but I'll hurry it along."

"I've got a better idea. Let me take us all out for supper."

"No, that costs too much."

"You've had a hard day. You need to relax. And I need a woman to talk to."

She smiled. "All right, let me change clothes first."

I returned to the living room and waited.

Jim was in the backyard climbing the cherry tree to see if anything was ripe yet.

Her son Russel came into the house and saw me. He was small for his age, and he wore the thickest glasses I'd ever seen in my life. He was awkward. I figured he went through life being in everybody's way. I wondered if he ever really knew what was going on around him.

"Hello," I said. "You must be Russel."

He nodded and left to go talk to his mother.

Poor Russel, I thought. I'll bet kids make fun of him at school.

Kellie returned. She'd made an effort to look clean, but not much effort into looking attractive. No makeup. No lipstick. No jewelry.

We asked the boys where they wanted to go and they said McDonald's.

We took the food to a park and let our kids play on the swings while we talked.

She was younger than me by a year. She'd been raised in Idaho and had met her future husband, Steve, during her first semester at BYU. They'd married in the spring of her freshman year. She'd quit school to help him get through. He never did. He died in an automobile accident. She hadn't dated anyone since then. I asked her why, and she said that she and Steve had been married forever.

I didn't understand that.

Her main goal was to finish her education so she could get a better-paying job. So far she'd saved enough money to take one night course next semester.

Her drive for an education reminded me of Pamela, and that was not particularly good for our relationship.

Steve hadn't carried any life insurance, so it was all up to her now. I admired her for making the best of a difficult situation.

When she smiled, which happened only occasionally, I loved the sunshine of her face. With a little more money for clothes, with makeup, and with time to get over the ache of losing her husband, she could be attractive to men. But I wasn't sure if she'd ever want that again.

The next day Ben and I got together in his office to do a read-through of the script. After an hour of mutual frustration, he finally shook his head. "I'm sorry, Michael, but it just isn't right."

"What's wrong with it?"

"I wish I could be more specific. I just know it's not right." He paused. "Before you did Carl Sandburg, did you do any research on him?"

"Yes."

He looked at his calendar. "Look, we've still got time before we start shooting. How about if you do research on Jesus? Take your time and then come back and we'll try it again, okay?"

I went to the library and spent the afternoon reading some of the books about Jesus. It seemed impossible to read through the large stack I found there. And even if I did, I'd read enough to know that they didn't agree with one another. So how could I know which one was right?

At five I went to pick up Jim. When I got there, I was surprised to notice that Kellie had eye makeup on. She looked much better.

"Do you know anything about Jesus?" I asked her.

"Yes, I do. Why?"

"Ben asked me to find out all I can about him. Any ideas of where to look?"

"What do you want to know?"

"Something to base a characterization on. Try acting the part of someone who's described to you only as glorious. I need something besides superlatives."

"I know a place you can go. It's in Salt Lake. Will you take Russel and me there sometime?"

"How about now? I'll treat us all to supper. How would that be?"

She smiled. "I never turn down an offer for a free supper."

* * * * *

Our destination was the Visitors Center on Temple Square in Salt Lake City. While I guided Moby Dick down the interstate at forty miles an hour, she looked over the script and gave me some hints.

Jim and Russel sat in the back seat, not even speaking to each other. I think Jim felt Russel was beneath him.

After we found a place to park, we started through the Visitors Center, looking at the posters and listening to the presentations. And then we started up a long sloping ramp. I was busy trying to make sure we had the boys with us, looking back and telling Jim to quit fooling around and catch up with us, all the time walking backwards up the ramp.

Then I turned and there it was, the statue of the *Christus*. His hands seemed to be reaching out to me.

I froze in my tracks.

"Are you all right?" Kellie asked.

I stood there, transfixed by that face. His eyes seemed to be looking directly at me. I felt how totally wrong it was for me to even think about playing the part of Jesus in the movie. What right did I have to represent him? None at all.

"You go ahead," I muttered. "I'll meet you when you're through." I turned and fled.

When I got to the first floor, I sat on a bench and tried to calm down. A few minutes later she came and sat next to me. "I took Jim and Russel to a presentation about the pioneers. Is something wrong?"

"I can't do the movie. Ben'll have to get someone else."

"If you didn't feel a little inadequate, I'd be worried. But don't worry, you'll do okay."

"You don't understand." I looked at my hands. "How can these hands be his hands? It'd be like mocking God. I'm not that good of a person."

"Nobody is, Michael. But he loves us anyway."

She reached over and touched my arm. "Have you ever thought about praying for help?"

"I don't know how to pray."

"I can teach you."

"I'm not sure I want to learn."

"Michael, you can't play the part of Jesus if you don't learn to pray."

I paused. "All right. Can you teach me?"

She talked to a supervisor, who agreed to let us use his office for a few minutes. We rounded up our kids and went in and closed the door. She helped me through my first prayer.

It was the first time in his life that Jim had ever had a kneeling family prayer. He wasn't impressed. "We won't be doing much more of this while we're in Utah, will we?"

After that we all went outside and looked at the flowers.

A young woman ran up to Kellie and cried out, "Kellie, is that you? I haven't seen you since we graduated from high school!"

"Marlis!" Kellie cried out.

They threw their arms around each other. Marlis introduced her husband and then turned to me. "And this must be your husband and your two little kids. They're adorable."

"Oh, he's not my husband," Kellie said. "He's just a friend. My husband died last year."

Her smile vanished. "I'm terribly sorry. I didn't know. Are these your boys?"

"One is mine and one is his," she said.

"Oh."

"I'm his," Jim said so there'd be no mistake.

"My wife left me a few months ago to go to Boston to become a gynecologist," I said.

"Oh." She looked at me with a strange expression. A few minutes later, she and her husband moved away, still full of unanswered questions.

*   *   *   *   *

On the way home, I offered to pay Kellie triple what she usually made in a week if she'd coach me about Jesus.

"Just think of it as a job," I said.

She finally agreed. When we got to her home, she phoned and made arrangements for a friend of hers to fill in for her the next week at the day-care center.

The next morning I picked her up and we drove to the Wilkinson Center at BYU and rented an office room for a week—charging it all to Ben.

We sat down opposite each other across a conference table. She'd brought scriptures and reference books with her.

"All right," I said. "What was Jesus really like? I need details."

"We know that he was a carpenter until he was about thirty years old. I think his hands had callouses from working, and his arms and shoulders were strong and muscular.

"He was the best that a man can be. Physically strong, and yet his feelings ran the full range of human emotion. He showed anger when he threw the moneychangers from the temple. He raged against the hypocrisy of the Pharisees, and yet he openly wept with compassion at other times. He never concealed his emotions. When he was angry, he let it out. When he was impatient with the apostles, he chastised them. But no matter what his emotion, he was always in control."

She turned to one of her books. "Here's a guideline he's given for temperament." She started reading. " 'No power or influence can or ought to be maintained by virtue of the priesthood, only by persuasion, by long-suffering, by gentleness and meekness, and by love unfeigned; by kindness, and pure knowledge, . . . reproving betimes with sharpness, when moved upon by the Holy Ghost; and then showing forth afterwards an increase of love toward him whom thou hast reproved.' "

"Does that describe how he was?" I asked.

"Yes, I think so. We know that he did sometimes reprove with sharpness." She turned to her Bible. "Listen to this. 'Now do ye Pharisees make clean the outside of the cup and the platter; but your inward part is full of ravening and wickedness.' Or think about when he drove out the moneychangers. Nobody even tried to stop him. They stood in awe of his manhood and power and the righteousness of the action.''

I took some notes. ''Okay, let's move on. One of the first scenes is Jesus changing water into wine.'' I thumbed through my script. ''His mother says to him, 'They have no wine.' And Jesus says, 'Woman, what have I to do with thee? mine hour is not yet come.' '' I read the passage as if Jesus was angry at his mother for bothering him.

''That's not the way it happened,'' she said. She turned to her Bible and read a slightly different passage. But the main difference was how she read it. Instead of angrily as I'd done, she showed a Jesus who was deeply respectful toward his mother. '' 'Woman, what wilt thou have me do for thee? that will I do; for mine hour is not yet come.' ''

I paused. ''How do you know he said it like that?''

''It's from the Joseph Smith Translation,'' she said.

Even though I'd been through at least part of the Visitors Center, I still didn't catch on. I figured it was just another version of the Bible.

We worked until noon and then went to the cafeteria for lunch. Afterwards we took a walk around campus. We finally stopped in front of the administration building and sat down by a fountain.

''I wish I had a camera to catch the sun shining in your hair,'' I said.

She closed her eyes and sadly shook her head.

''Did I say something wrong?''

''It's just that Steve used to say that about my hair—how good it looked in the sun.''

For some reason that annoyed me. ''Well, sure he did. Any guy'd tell you that.''

She stared at me as if I'd just slapped her face.

''Look, Kellie, I'm tired of us telling each other we're sorry. Can we just say it one more time and be done with it? I'm really sorry your husband died. And I'm sorry my wife divorced me and that my dad died. But it happened. Now you and I are here together for the next few days. We're still young and now we're both single, and if I happen to notice the way your hair shines in the sun, I'm going to tell you about it. It doesn't mean I'm trying to romance you. It just means I'm alive. Okay?''

"There's no way you can understand how I feel," she said.

"How do you feel?"

"Like I'm still married to Steve."

"You're not though."

"I was married in the temple."

"I don't care where you were married. You can't be married to a man who's dead."

"You don't know about our church. In the temple you can get married for time and eternity."

"You keep saying that, but what does it mean?"

"It means that even after Steve died, I'm still married."

"Are you telling me you can't ever marry anyone else?"

She paused. "No. I can marry again, but my second marriage will last only until I die."

"All right, if you can get married again, then that means you're not married now, doesn't it?"

She didn't want to talk about it. "We should get back to work. An hour lunch break is all I'm used to."

I was furious with her for treating this as an employer-employee relationship. "And as your employer," I grumbled, "I certainly respect that. It's so hard to get good help these days."

Even by the time we reached the office, I was still fuming.

"I think we should have a prayer before we start again," she said.

"No. I'm not paying you to pray."

"Michael, I don't think we can talk about the Savior with all this tension in the room."

"Tension? What tension? I don't know what you're talking about. Why should there be tension between us? Go ahead where you left off."

She opened her Bible, started to read, and then stopped. "I can't do it."

"Why not?"

"There's a bad feeling between us. I think we should talk about it."

"Why do women have to be so emotional?" I raged. "Look, I don't want to talk about it. You want to know why? Because talking to you is like walking on eggshells."

Then I stormed out of the office.

When I returned a few minutes later, she was patiently waiting for me. "You didn't walk out on me," I said.

"Did you think I would?"

"Women always leave me. Why didn't you?"

She shrugged her shoulders. "I really need the money."

It was such an honest thing to say that it made me smile. "Listen to me. I want us to be friends. It's true I'm paying you for your help, but I don't want you to think of it as a job. That's mainly my gripe, okay?"

She looked at me. "Okay, but I still think we should pray."

She knelt down and closed her eyes.

From then on, we always started each session off with a prayer. The first few times I kept my eyes open so I could gaze at her face. It was nice to look at her without her getting nervous by the attention.

But eventually I too began to close my eyes.

*   *   *   *   *

We continued the next day.

"It says Jesus blessed the little children," I said. "How do you picture that?"

"Mothers brought him their children, but the disciples tried to give him time to rest. Besides, they didn't see any need for Jesus to be involved with children, because they knew that children are free from sin until they reach the age of accountability. But Jesus loved little children, and he asked the disciples to let the mothers come ahead with their little ones.

"I picture him picking up a little boy and setting him on his lap, and asking him what his name was. And maybe the boy would give him a special gift, like an extra-smooth rock he'd found along the way from his home, or a flower picked just for him.

"Then came time for the blessing. Jesus would put his hands on the boy's head and call him by name and bless him to grow up healthy and strong and to love the truth. Maybe he'd tell him to always remember that when he was a boy he'd seen the Kingdom of God come to earth.

"He gave a personal blessing for each boy or girl, and then returned the child back to its mother. It was a sweet time for him and for the children."

"How do you know all this?" I asked.

"Once I had a husband who gave blessings to my boy."

*   *   *   *   *

Each day we went through details of the script. I practiced my lines for her. After work I often took the four of us out to supper or she'd cook something for us.

"Are you going to marry her?" Jimmy asked me one night.

"Of course not." I paused. "But if I did, what would you think about that?"

"I like Mom better."

"Sure, well, don't worry about it. Kellie and I are just friends."

*   *   *   *   *

Kellie asked us if we'd like to go fishing with her and Russel on Saturday.

I said of course, thinking I'd impress her with my expertise.

We drove to a reservoir and rented a boat. We rowed out a ways near where some other boats were anchored. She showed us how Steve used to bait the hooks.

"Russel is such a good fisherman," she said. "He always catches the first fish."

She threw Russel's line into the water first and then fixed the other poles.

Just after she tossed Jim's line in the water, Russel caught the first fish. We all cheered Russel on while he reeled in. She got up and netted it by herself.

While we were waiting for some more action, she gave us cinnamon rolls she'd baked that morning.

Jim caught the second fish. It weighed two pounds.

"This is fun!" he shouted. "Dad and I never caught fish like this!"

I blushed.

We caught five fish, and then Kellie let Jim try his hand at rowing.

We quit at eleven. Kellie showed me a quick way to clean fish, and then we had a picnic lunch of potato salad, lemonade, fried chicken, and chocolate cake.

After we got home that night, Jim said he couldn't see why Russel's mom said he was such a great fisherman, when the only reason he caught the first fish was because his line was in the water before anyone else's, and he really didn't do anything but reel in the line anyway.

"Jim, it's important that Russel feel that he's good at something."

"Well, he is good at something."

"What?" I asked.

"Tripping over the cracks in the sidewalk," he said with a smirk.

*   *   *   *   *

"I want to have an official date with you," I said the next day. She swallowed. "Oh."

"A dinner and then a movie. What do you say?"

She frowned. "I wouldn't be good company for you."

"It'll just be practice for when some rich guy comes along."

"I don't have anything to wear."

"You wear nice outfits to church, don't you? Wear one of those."

She paused, then said quietly, "Wait here and I'll show you what I mean."

A minute later she brought some clothes from her bedroom. She showed me a nice dress.

"Sure, that's fine," I said. "Wear that."

"I wore this the first time on my honeymoon."

"Oh."

She carefully laid it aside and picked up another. "And this one I wore the night Steve proposed to me."

She picked up a black dress. "I wore this to Steve's funeral." She stopped. "Do you see what I mean? I don't have anything to wear."

"Get rid of them, Kellie."

She shook her head. "I can't do that."

"I'll buy you a complete new wardrobe—whatever you want. It's not good for you to have those clothes here. Steve's dead. You've got to move on with your life."

"I'm trying, but it's so hard."

"You believe Steve is somewhere now, don't you?"

"Yes."

"Do you think he wants you torturing yourself this way?"

She looked at me. "No."

"Then let me help you." I walked over to the clothes, bundled them up in my arms, and walked out of her house.

By the time I reached my car she'd figured out what I was going to do. She ran out to stop me. I drove away, leaving her standing in the street, calling after me to stop.

I drove to a Deseret Industries store and donated the clothes to them. Just before leaving, I had a clerk look at the dresses and tell me what sizes I should get for Kellie. Then I went to a woman's clothing store and bought her five new dresses.

An hour later when I went to her house and knocked, she wouldn't answer the door. I left the clothes on her front step and went around to get Jim. He was in the backyard doing chin-ups on the top bar of their swing.

We drove to our house and I fixed supper.

"She cried a lot after you left," he said.

"Eat your beans."

Later that evening she phoned me.

"What did you do with my dresses?" she asked.

"I gave them away."

There was a long painful silence. Then, "I know you were only trying to help."

"That's right."

"I tried on the dresses that you bought me," she said. "They're very nice."

"It's no big deal—they were on sale."

"You shouldn't spend money on me."

"When I have money, I spend it."

"I have one of the dresses on now. Do you want to come over and see me in it?"

"Yes, I'd like that very much."

A few minutes later I knocked on the door of her place. She opened the door. She had put makeup on and was wearing perfume. She was wearing the cream-colored dress with lace at the neck.

"Why are you staring at me?" she asked.

"I didn't know how beautiful you are."

"Thank you."

It was true she was stunning, but it was the beauty of a fragile china doll. I felt that the slightest jar would cause her to break in a million pieces.

We sat down in her living room. The phonograph was playing slow songs.

"Would you like a glass of lemonade?" she asked.

"Yes, thank you."

She brought out two glasses of lemonade from the kitchen.

We were acting out a scene, but the only problem was, I didn't know what part she wanted me to play.

"Let me turn off this overhead light," she said. "It makes the room look so bare when it's on." She turned off the light, leaving just a small lamp on top of the TV to give us light. She sat down beside me, desperately clutching her glass of lemonade.

She looked at me. "I can see why you decided to become an actor."

"Why's that?"

"You're very good-looking." She closed her eyes as if it had been an ordeal even to get the words out.

There was a long silence.

"Thank you," I finally said.

"You probably think I say that to all the guys. But I don't."

"Kellie, I know that."

"Tell me, do you like to dance?" she asked.

"Sure."

"I used to belong to a ballroom dance group at BYU."

"Oh."

"It's good exercise. Do you want to dance now?"

"Okay."

I stood up and put out my hand to help her up, but she suddenly turned away and shook her head. She started turning her wedding band back and forth on her finger. "I'm sorry. I guess I don't want to dance after all. You know, I've never seen it rain so much for this time of year." She paused. "Michael, do you think I'm attractive?" she asked.

"Very."

"Even though I'm a widow?"

"Yes."

"There's a waltz called the 'Merry Widow' waltz, isn't there? That's what I am tonight, isn't it? The merry widow. I wanted to dress up for you so you'd get your money's worth for buying me clothes."

I was embarrassed she'd said that. "Kellie, please, this is turning out all wrong. I think I'd better go home now."

Her voice was thin and high. "I've put on a little weight, but I'm getting down to what I used to weigh before I got married. It's like a boxer trying to make a comeback. Someday I'll be back in the swing of things, going on dates, flirting."

She tried to smile, but the pain on her face made it come out all wrong. "I've read about coping with being a widow. I need to meet new people, make friends, get out of the house, get used to men again. They say it's hard at first, but you just have to do it. Maybe they're right. I'm still young. There's other men, hundreds of them, to replace . . ."

She stopped, her emotions on the ragged edge, teetering between control and breakdown. ". . . hundreds of men to replace the only man I'll ever love."

The charade was over. She buried her face on the arm of the couch and cried.

I tried to put my arm around her but she shook it off. "Kellie, what can I do for you?"

She turned to face me. Tears were streaming down her face. "You can't do anything. You want to know why? Because I don't care about you, not at all. And I never will."

"I want to help if I can," I said.

"All right, you're an actor. Can you be like Steve? Can you say the things he used to say? Can you smile at me the way he used to? Because if you can't, then you're no use to me. Can't you see? I'm stranded here without him. Why couldn't I have died with him? He's the only man I'll ever love. What am I going to do? Nobody knows how much I miss him."

She ran to her bedroom and closed the door.

Her crying had awakened Russel. He came out, wearing pajamas with pictures of bear clowns. He saw me in the dimly lit living room, still holding my untouched glass of lemonade.

"Sometimes she cries at night," he said. "Don't go away—she'll come out when she feels better."

"Thanks."

He went in to see her. He left the bedroom door open so that from where I sat in the living room, I could see them. She was lying face down on the bed, crying. He sat down on the bed next to her and patted her on the back, the way a mother does to her crying child. This time the roles were reversed.

"Mom, it's okay, don't cry."

It was the first time I'd seen her bedroom because she always kept the door closed in the daytime when I came to get Jimmy. There were still two pillows on the bed. One of them must have been Steve's. A blue bathrobe, too big to be hers, hung on a hook in the closet where maybe Steve had hung it after his shower on the day he died. Several pictures of the two of them were on the wall, and a wedding certificate from a temple hung there too. Library books were stacked on the bedstand. I wondered if she read late at night when she couldn't sleep.

I could see her clothes in the closet, and a bare spot where Steve's clothes had hung.

I knew I was invading her privacy, but I couldn't force myself to look away. I wanted to know every detail of that room.

I thought about going with Russel back to his room and tucking him into bed and then telling him that it was better for his mom to cry than it was to always try and hold it in, and that he could cry too whenever he needed to. And then I'd gently close his door after me and go see Kellie. I wanted to wipe the tears from her cheek and hold her in my arms while she cried. I wanted to tell her that someday things would be better. I wanted to be with her.

But I knew I couldn't go, because there were other emotions besides brotherly concern that would persuade me to enter that room.

She was a beautiful woman.

And so I stayed put and watched the two of them struggling to cope.

A few minutes later he said, "Mom, Michael's waiting for you. You'd better go see him."

She sat up and saw the open door and realized I'd been watching all along. Quietly she asked Russel to close the door.

A few minutes later she came out. "I'm sorry," she said. "I didn't know it would be so hard. It was a mistake. I'm not ready for this yet."

"Maybe not, but don't stop now. You need to start dating again. You can practice on me until somebody better comes along."

"I'm no fun for you."

"It's all right. I'm not in such great shape myself. Besides, what are friends for, right?"

"Well, I'll think about it, but now you'd better go. I need another favor. Can you take that record and get rid of it for me?"

She said it was a record with memories, that sometimes Steve had played it at night for just the two of them after Russel was asleep.

When I got home, I carefully set the record on the curb and stepped on it. It broke into many pieces. I picked them up one by one and threw them as hard as I could into the darkness of that bleak night.

CHAPTER   SIX

The next day when we returned to our work, she wore what must have been her least attractive skirt and blouse. We didn't talk about what had happened the night before.

We were to the point in our studies where we needed to talk about the crucifixion.

"Tell me how you picture it," I said.

Her voice was subdued. "People often picture it as some epic stage production. It wasn't that. It was an innocent man suffering a cruel and painful death.

"While he was on the cross, the only way he could breathe was by standing on the nail through his feet. He did that until the pain was unbearable and then he'd collapse, which put strain on the wounds in his hands and wrists. But then, in order to breathe again, the whole cycle had to be repeated.

"Think what it must have been like from his point of view, looking down from the cross, seeing the hardened Roman soldiers. For them, inflicting painful death was a skill they prided themselves on. His enemies came and mocked him, saying that if he came down from the cross, they'd believe. And even the few friends who did show up felt in their hearts that he'd failed.

"Think about how he felt as he gazed on his mother's face, knowing full well that she shared his every pain, that his every gasp tore her apart.

"Most of his clothes had been taken by the Roman soldiers. I picture his white skin standing out against the dull dark wood of the cross. Did his mother understand that this was necessary? How could she? All she knew was that her precious son was being tortured to death. I wonder if there were drops of blood falling from his wounds upon the dusty ground, and if his mother watched those drops as they fell. That poor woman must have nearly died from the heartache she felt.

"In my mind I see the nails in his hands and feet, and his chest heaving, and his muscles throbbing in spasms. He ached so much. And he was all alone. There was nobody to share the burden. Even the heavens withdrew. It was his burden alone to bear."

We sat without speaking for several seconds. Then she went on.

"He said a few words while he was on the cross. It wasn't something he said just to fulfill prophecy. All that he said was the natural result of his suffering.

"What I'm trying to say is, focus on details: his face, his hands, his feet, his breathing, the texture of the roughened wood. It was not a religious pageant. It was murder, it was painful, it was humiliating, and nobody in the crowd had any idea that it was necessary. They figured it could've been avoided if he'd just used a little more tact, or if he hadn't come to Jerusalem for the Passover, or if he'd been more polite to the Sanhedrin, or if he'd gotten himself a good lawyer, or if he'd fled from the soldiers who came to arrest him, or any number of things. How could they understand that this was the very reason he came to the earth? To his friends on that terrible day, he was an embarrassment, an agonizing failure."

She reached for her scriptures. "Michael, I added to his suffering on that day."

"How?"

"Because he carried the burden of our sins. Mine and yours too. He suffered for our sins not only on the cross but also in the Garden of Gethsemane."

"Why would he do that?"

"So we won't have to."

"I didn't ask him to."

"I know," she said, "but he did it for us, and we all added to the price he had to pay."

She turned to a passage in one of her books. "Here's what he said years later about his suffering in Gethsemane. 'Which suffering caused myself, even God, the greatest of all, to tremble because of pain, and to bleed at every pore, and to suffer both body and spirit—and would that I might not drink the bitter cup, and shrink. Nevertheless, glory be to the Father, and I partook and finished my preparations unto the children of men.'

"Michael, it's so sad to think of him there on that cross. Can we go just beyond that? I want to tell you what happened the instant after he died. Just a minute while I find it." She turned to one of her books. "Okay, here it is. 'And there were gathered together in one place an innumerable company of the spirits of the just, who had been faithful in the testimony of Jesus while they lived in mortality. . . . I beheld that they were filled with joy and gladness, and were rejoicing because the day of their deliverance was at hand. . . . While this vast multitude waited and conversed, rejoicing in the hour of their deliverance from the chains of death, the Son of God appeared, declaring liberty to the captives who had been faithful.'

"Isn't it good to know that at the same instant his body slumped on the cross, he was welcomed by noble men and women who loved him with all their hearts?"

"I've never heard that before."

"I know." She paused as if she was about to tell me something else, but I interrupted her.

"What about the resurrection?" I asked. "Do you really think that happened?"

"Yes, I know that it did. His body and his spirit were reunited, and he walked out of the tomb with a resurrected body of flesh and bone. He was seen by thousands of people over the course of the next few days, and they all testified to what they had seen."

"But maybe he wasn't really dead, maybe just wounded, and then he regained consciousness and walked out of the tomb and told everybody he had come back to life."

"No, that's not the way it happened."

I could see she wasn't going to back down.

"Everyone who dies will be resurrected. It's a free gift, given to us by Jesus. I think about that now more than ever. I can't wait until I see Steve, alive again. I've dreamed about it ever since the accident—the time when I'll be in Steve's arms again."

"Sounds real nice," I said as enthusiastically as I could.

CHAPTER SEVEN

The next day I took Kellie to dinner at a Japanese restaurant in Salt Lake City. We took off our shoes upon entering the small private bamboo room they gave us. She looked more beautiful than ever before. I told her so, and, almost reluctantly, she thanked me.

I asked her how she knew about the restaurant, and she told me Steve had taken her there once.

The waitress brought us a relish dish and water and a menu and then left.

I asked if this was the same booth she and Steve had had.

She said she wasn't sure, but it might be.

We quit talking.

She said she knew she wasn't any good for me. She said she thought it would be best if I quit seeing her. She said it was too soon after Steve's death for her to be seeing a man. Besides that, maybe it would be better if we didn't see each other so much because I wasn't a member of her church.

I asked if she'd ever marry someone who wasn't a Mormon, and she said no. I asked why she had gone to so much trouble lately looking nice for me if she wasn't interested.

She said she just wanted to show her appreciation for my helping her.

I asked if that's all there was to it.

She said she was sorry if I'd gotten the wrong message, but she would never allow herself to get serious with me.

Allow herself? That's what she said. Allow herself. As if I was some terrible temptation that must be avoided at all costs.

When it came time to order, I sarcastically told her to go ahead and order the same thing she'd had with Steve there before, so she could sit and bawl through the entire meal.

She said she thought I was being insensitive.

I told her I thought she was an emotional cripple, incapable of maintaining any kind of mature adult relationship.

She said if I felt that way, maybe we'd better just end the evening right there and then.

I said that would suit me just fine.

I gave the waitress some money for the carrot sticks and we left.

Outside, the wind rustled wrappers in the gutters as we walked silently back to the car. A storm was coming.

The car wouldn't start. I got out and opened up the hood to see if I could fix it.

The rain started to pour down.

"You should get inside," Kellie said to me from the car.

"Don't tell me what to do! Okay?"

I was getting drenched, though, and so a minute later I swallowed my pride and jumped back in the car.

"Stupid carburetor," I raged, slamming my fist against the steering wheel. "The first thing I'm going to do when I get some money is get me a decent car, and the second thing'll be to find a normal woman to date."

"Good. I think that's exactly what you should do," she said.

I swore and angrily hit the steering wheel with my fist.

While lightning ravaged the sky and the rain rolled in sheets down the windshield, we sat there like stones. I had my arms folded tightly around me and was staring straight ahead.

I'll never know why she did it, but suddenly she leaned over and kissed me on the cheek.

I was shocked. "What did you do that for?"

She smiled. "Just to say thanks. I know this is hard for both of us, but I think it's good we're trying to work through it, don't you?"

Uncertain, I slowly put my hand next to hers on the car seat. She completed the action by putting her hand on mine.

We were actually holding hands. All my pent-up anger seemed to drain away.

I asked if she was still hungry and she said yes, so I took a blanket from the back seat and we held it over our heads while we ran back to the restaurant. They seated us in a different room.

I decided to let her open up about Steve so there wouldn't always be this wall between us. And so while we ate, I asked about him.

She told me how they met, the dates they had at BYU, their wedding in the Provo Temple, and where they went on their honeymoon. She described their first apartment in Provo. She told me how tight things were the first year, and about her getting pregnant when they had the least amount of money, and how Steve said it'd all work out, and how when his uncle died, Steve got enough of an inheritance to allow them to make a down payment on their tiny house.

She told about Russel's birth, and how Steve spent hours playing with his son. And how devastated they'd been when they first realized how bad Russel's eyesight was. She told me how Steve had to quit school for a year and a half to earn money to pay for some of Russel's medical bills. And how long and drawn-out college seemed to them, and how broke they were most of the time.

Steve had to go to school in the day and work at nights, and he never got enough sleep. One night he didn't come home from work on time. And then the phone call, saying that he'd been hurt and could she go to the hospital. When she got there, they said he'd been dead all along, but they hadn't wanted to tell her over the phone.

When we left the restaurant, the car still wouldn't start, but at least the rain had stopped. I opened the hood and had her hold the flashlight while I worked on the carburetor.

"I saw a car the other day," I said while I worked. "It's a Corvette. It's a few years old, but it's in good shape. I've got enough money for the down payment, so this weekend I might go trade in this wreck. How'd you like driving around in a red sports car?"

"That'd be nice," she said. "Where did you learn how to fix cars?"

"From my dad."

"Do you miss him?"

I looked up at her. "Sometimes I talk to him in my mind."

"About what?"

"Oh, I don't know. Little things mostly."

"I talk to Steve sometimes," she admitted.

I smiled. "We're quite a pair, aren't we."

On the way home, she told me how much she had loved being in his arms, how sometimes late at night she cried when the loneliness got too great. She told me it was better to cry in the night because then Russel didn't know.

"He knows," I said. "The night I bought you those dresses, he told me that's what you do."

"Poor Russel."

"Is there anything else you want to tell me about Steve?"

"He was my friend, my sweetheart, my husband, the father of my son, and he was close to God."

Having her tell about him had brought us closer. Now I shared her grief. On the doorstep I held her in my arms. Just as I was about to kiss her, she turned away and said she thought she'd better go in.

*   *   *   *   *

I met with Ben the next day. I read for him again. "I can't believe how much you've improved. There's so much more depth and sensitivity than you had before."

"Kellie's helped me a lot."

"Great."

"Ben, she's your cousin. Was Steve as wonderful as she says?"

"He was very good for her."

"You're a Mormon too, aren't you?" I asked.

"That's right."

"She talks about still being married to him. Is that what your church teaches?"

"She's single now, but after she dies, their marriage will continue. We believe a wedding in one of our temples lasts forever."

"But is it possible for her to remarry?"

"Yes, she can be married again, but she can be married to only one man in the eternities."

"Just for the sake of argument, suppose I joined her church, and we got married—who would have her after we died?"

"She'd have to decide which of the two she'd prefer to have in the hereafter. Why do you ask? Are you really that serious about her?"

I shrugged my shoulders. "Probably not. If I wanted to get married again, which I don't, I'd go out and find someone without so much emotional baggage, and I definitely wouldn't go looking for a Mormon."

"Oh, I don't know," he said with a smile. "We're not so bad."

CHAPTER EIGHT

It's a zoo, I thought, the day before the actual filming began.

For the next few weeks extras would be showing up at five in the morning and staying until sunset; a catering truck would be bringing lunch to feed the cast and crew. On location there were fifty head of sheep, six goats, and a crate of pigeons; two working Galilean fishing boats; the exterior shells of the village of Nazareth; several Roman soldiers with horses, spears, and insignia; a large semitrailer containing a diesel engine to run all the electrical equipment; cables running every which way; and two camels with their drivers.

In other words, a zoo.

*   *   *   *   *

The cameras were rolling. As Jesus, I walked along a dusty road accompanied by a large crowd.

A blind man asked a passerby what the noise was all about. He was told that Jesus of Nazareth was passing. He began to call out for Jesus.

"Hold your peace, you old fool!" one of the crowd warned the man.

If he keeps calling out like that, the man in the crowd thought, then the Master will hear him, and we'll have to stop again. At this rate we'll never get there before nightfall. Who knows how many robbers are waiting up there just around the bend for anyone foolish enough to travel at night. And why do we have to keep stopping for any scum that happens to cry for help?

The man in the crowd wanted to have them all rush past that beggar, but Jesus heard and stopped.

With the cameras going, I looked down at the man. Scabs covered his face and eyes.

I found myself wondering what Jesus saw in that blind beggar. What difference can it make if there's one less blind beggar? None at all. The world doesn't concern itself with blind beggars. It makes no difference.

Why did Jesus do it? He could have just walked past. Nobody would have even thought about it if he had. Maybe it was because he saw something remarkable about the man. But what?

What if it wasn't just this particular beggar—what if it was everyone he met.

"Cut!" Ben called out. "Michael, what's the delay here? You're supposed to touch the man's eyes and heal him."

The next time I did it right. But for that tiny instant I had felt as if I were looking at someone the way Jesus did, with overwhelming, unconditional love.

It was a strange experience.

*   *   *   *   *

After work I dropped by Kellie's house to get Jim. When I walked in, I saw Russel practicing the violin in the living room. He was wearing green slacks that were a little too large for him. They must have been given to him by neighbors or church members. One cuff was rolled up, the other wasn't. He stood there with his battered, borrowed violin, his eyes nearly touching the sheet music, straining to see the notes on the page, his foot clumsily tapping out the beat. His eyes appeared larger than normal through his thick glasses.

And then suddenly I was seeing Russel through someone else's eyes—someone who loved him with all his heart.

The way Jesus loved him.

The way Steve loved him.

A number of impressions flashed through my mind. A minute later, I knew I had to talk to Kellie. She was at the front door, just seeing off her last day-care child.

"I've got to talk to you in the backyard," I said.

She followed me.

"Why do you have Russel taking violin lessons?" I asked.

"It's something he can learn."

"He shouldn't be taking violin lessons."

"Why not?"

"Because kids already make fun of him. You think violin lessons help that? Russel should be learning karate, or something physically oriented like that."

"Steve used to talk about that too, but I don't know. You can see he's not very coordinated."

"That's why you pay somebody to give him lessons, so he'll get coordinated. Kellie, we've got to help him."

"I'm doing the best I can. The only reason he can take violin is because I trade off lessons for baby-sitting. I know you mean well, but I don't have money for karate lessons."

"I've got some money. Let me spend some of it on your son."

She looked at me suspiciously. "I thought you were going to buy a sports car with your money."

"Russel is more important."

"Are you saying that just to impress me?"

"No," I said.

"Then why?"

"I looked at Russel just now, and . . ." I stopped.

"What is it?"

"I don't know how to explain it. I want to help. Can't you let me help?"

She sighed. "I'm not proud anymore. I'll be grateful for anything you can do to help Russel."

I paused. "There's more but I'm not sure I should tell you."

"What is it?"

"I had a feeling, you'll think it's crazy . . ."

"Tell me."

"I think Steve wants me to help you with Russel."

She looked at me strangely.

I was embarrassed to even have said it, so I went back inside to talk to Russel.

"What's your name?" I asked him.

"Russel."

"No, I don't think so. You're a Rusty. Rusty Green. Come here, I want to test something." I took a newspaper and folded it in two and held it out for him. "All right, you've seen karate on TV, right? I want you to do a karate chop on this newspaper."

He made an awkward uncertain movement down with his fist. As soon as he made contact, I let the paper fall to the floor.

"All right! You've got talent. We've got to get you taking karate classes. In fact, we'll all start right away."

Rusty, Jim, and I drove to a karate training club and bought white uniforms and enrolled in lessons. What with the uniforms and the initiation fees for the three of us, and prepaying for a month of lessons, by the time we left, my down payment for a car was nearly gone.

Rusty wouldn't take the white karate warm-up suit off the rest of the day. In fact, Kellie told me he even slept in it.

The next day the three of us began our first karate lessons. It wasn't so much fighting as choreographing a dance step. We took lessons twice a week.

I took Rusty to an eye doctor and asked what more could be done for him. The doctor recommended a new lens material that would reduce the thickness of the lenses. We ordered a new pair of glasses. Instead of the sturdy plastic rims Rusty was wearing, I ordered a pair of wire frames that made him look like John Denver as a boy.

Sometimes when we practiced karate I called him Tiger. He seemed to like that.

CHAPTER NINE

Each day I poured everything I had into my portrayal of Jesus.

On Saturday we were filming out by Utah Lake. Ben had planned on shooting only in the morning, but we were delayed getting started. At first the wind was blowing too much, and then it rained. By eleven o'clock we still hadn't shot anything. Shortly before noon the weather improved and the wind died down.

We were about to start when an assistant director came up to Ben. "The extras were told it'd only be till noon."

"Tell 'em to bear with us," Ben said.

"You've got children out there, you've got old men and women, you ought to get 'em fed before very long."

Ben turned to someone else. "So where's the catering trucks?"

"You said we'd be working today just till noon. The trucks aren't coming."

"We've got to shoot this now. I don't want to wait another day."

"Maybe not, but I don't see what else you can do. People are getting hungry."

Ben sighed. "Call everybody together and we'll talk about it."

A minute later he took a portable P.A. system and read about the miracle of the loaves.

"People, we all have some food, don't we? I've got a couple of cans of food and some crackers in the car for emergencies. Some of you may have something else. Now let's see if we can forget our own selfish concerns, and go to our cars or trucks or campers, and take the food we have, and not hold back, and let's bring it all here to this table and see if we have enough to give us all at least something to eat for lunch. Look at that sky. It's perfect for what we need for this shot. Please, let's just see what happens when we open up our hearts the way Jesus taught."

People began filing off to their cars and trailers.

We watched them come back with their food and lay it on the table. Before long the table was full, and we had more to eat than if we'd had the catering trucks.

A few minutes later Ben asked someone to say a blessing on the food. After everyone had eaten, there was still food left over.

It was our own private miracle.

*   *   *   *   *

A few days later we were filming the scene where Jesus sits in a boat talking to the assembled multitudes on the shore. We'd scattered extras all over a steep hillside near the lake.

While I was speaking, one of the extras lost his footing and fell twenty feet.

"Cut!" Ben called out.

I jumped off the boat and ran to where the man had fallen. There was a large gash on his head where he'd hit a rock. He was unconscious.

A few minutes later an ambulance arrived and two paramedics came running down the incline to the shoreline to where the man was lying.

We quit for the day. I rode in with Ben to the hospital to see how the man was doing. He was still unconscious. His wife was there. She said they had five kids. Her husband had been laid off from his job at the steel mill, and he'd hired on as an extra hoping to bring in a little money.

A short time later two men showed up at the hospital. She called one of them Bishop, and the other Brother Mattson.

They closed the door. One of them poured a drop of oil on the man's head and then gently placed his hands on his head and said a prayer. Then they both placed their hands on the

man's head, and the one called Bishop promised the man that
he would recover fully.

It was the way the Savior did it, and, in fact, they did it in the
name of Jesus Christ.

Half an hour later the man came out of his coma.

I was stunned.

*   *   *   *   *

That night I told Kellie what had happened.

"I don't find that hard to believe."

"Well, I do. Why don't you?"

"Because the power Jesus had to heal the sick has been
restored to the earth. It's called priesthood. The men in the
church have it."

She told me about the restoration of the priesthood.

"Why didn't you talk to me about this earlier?"

"I didn't think you'd be interested."

"Not interested in the power to heal the sick? Of course I'm
interested. But I can't understand why you'd hold back. I
thought we were friends."

"I didn't want to push my beliefs on you."

I paused. "Maybe there's another reason. Maybe you wanted
an excuse not to get serious with me."

She sighed. "I don't know. Maybe so."

"Listen to me. I'm going to learn about this, and if it's true,
then I'm going to join, regardless of what happens between us."

I drove to Ben's home. "I want to learn about your church."

"When?"

"Right now."

He called around for some missionaries who were available
to come and teach me. After they finished their first discussion,
they got ready to pack up.

"Don't stop," I said.

The missionaries looked at each other. "But it's ten-thirty,"
one of them said.

"I don't care. Please go on."

They started in again. At eleven-thirty they pleaded with me to let them get some sleep. I gave in, but I made them promise to come to my house and teach me and Jim the next night.

* * * * *

That Sunday Jim and I went to church with Kellie and Rusty.

First we had church for an hour, then we had church for another hour, and then we had church again, for another hour. Three hours of church.

I started the day admiring the girls and women but ended it studying the men.

They were unusual men, almost apologetic in fulfilling their church responsibilities, feeling that there must be somebody more capable to do the job they'd been asked to do, but they went ahead as best they could.

In priesthood meeting, they asked for and got volunteers to visit the hospital during the week. They needed someone with a pickup who could help a family move on Wednesday. And did anybody know of a job, because Brother Jones was out of work. The softball team was going to practice on Wednesday because Thursday was their last game and they'd lost five in a row. Wasn't there anybody in the group who could pitch?

And then there was a lesson. The teacher told about a time recently when he lost his temper with his wife, and how he had to go back and apologize. Another told about a decision he'd made to cut down long hours at work so he'd have more time to spend with his kids, and that eventually it meant he got passed over for a promotion, but it was okay, he said, because he could get by without the extra money, but he couldn't get by without his kids knowing he loved them.

I found myself thinking that if these men hold God's power as they say they do, then it is a power different than what the world is used to. It is a gentle power, a power that can work only if a man is not trying to look powerful.

As I sat there in priesthood meeting, I had to keep reminding myself that the men in that room claimed to possess the power to heal the sick and raise the dead and give sight to the blind. And yet there wasn't one of them that looked like Charlton Heston as Moses in *The Ten Commandments.*

Yes, I was puzzled by the men I met in priesthood meeting.

"How did you like it?" I asked Jim.

"It was way too long."

"Other than that, how was it?"

"They made us sing dumb songs."

"What was dumb about 'em?"

"They were girl's songs. One of 'em was, 'When I'm helping, I'm happy, and I sing as I go, 'cause I love to help Mother, for we all love her so.' "

"You used to help Mom, didn't you?"

"Sure, but what good did it do? She still left, didn't she?"

*   *   *   *   *

I was fasting the day we shot the crucifixion scene. It was a sobering experience to retrace his agony on the cross.

After we finished for the day, I went by Kellie's to get Jim. She could see I was exhausted, and so she asked if I'd stay for supper.

"I'm not hungry."

"Michael, you've got to eat."

I sat down at the kitchen table while she worked. "They put nails in his hands and feet," I said.

"I know."

"And people came and spit in his face."

"It must have been awful for him."

At supper I looked at the food on my plate and told her I wasn't hungry.

After supper, she asked if I'd like to go for a drive with her.

She drove us up Provo Canyon. After we got back to town, she pulled up to a drive-in, hoping to entice me with a root beer.

A girl came to our car to get our order. Kellie ordered two root beers. The girl left.

"Do you see that girl's face?" I asked.

"What about it?"

"There's something bothering her."

"Maybe she's just having a bad day."

A few minutes later the girl brought the root beer.

I got out of the car and walked over to her. "Something's wrong, isn't it?" I took a step toward her.

She turned to Kellie. "You keep him away or I'm calling the cops."

The girl walked quickly away from me.

I got in the car again.

"Here's your root beer," Kellie said, handing me a frosty mug.

"I'm sure there's something bothering her."

"Michael, you've got to loosen up. You're scaring people."

"But don't you see—Jesus would know what to say, what to tell her."

"But Michael, you aren't him."

"I know, but I want to be like him."

It was the first time I'd admitted it.

I loved him.

*　　*　　*　　*　　*

"We've got a slight problem," Ben said a few days later.

"What's that?"

"I've been comparing what we shot earlier with yesterday's footage. There's a difference in the way you're playing the role now. We may have to reshoot some of the earlier scenes. There's so much more depth to what you're doing now. What's going on here?"

"I've been reading the Book of Mormon."

*　　*　　*　　*　　*

When I first began to learn about Jesus, I would discover a trait of his and use that to describe him in my mind. For instance, when I first read the parables, I came away thinking, okay, Jesus was a master teacher. We can leave it at that or we can go deeper. We can stay on the surface for an entire lifetime. "Jesus? Oh yes, I know about him, He was a master teacher."

We can leave it at that, or we can go deeper.

Because I wanted so much to make him come alive on the screen, I went deeper. What I found is that there are layers to our understanding of him. And when we first reach the next deeper level, we say, oh yes, now I know what he is really like.

Again, we can leave it at that, or we can go deeper.

But we never come to the end of him, we never make a true measure of the man, because he is like a sky with no horizon. As wonderful as you can imagine him to be, he is a thousand times more wonderful.

I'd spent hours poring over the New Testament, searching for just one more insight about him. And so when I discovered the Book of Mormon, it was like finding a dear friend, because the purpose of the Book of Mormon is to testify about Jesus.

It was in the Book of Mormon where I read that after his resurrection, Jesus came down from heaven to stand before a group of people in the New World. He began by saying, "Behold, I am Jesus Christ, whom the prophets testified shall come into the world. And behold, I am the light and the life of the world; and I have drunk out of that bitter cup which the Father hath given me, and have glorified the Father in taking upon me the sins of the world, in the which I have suffered the will of the Father in all things from the beginning."

The crowd fell to their knees.

" 'Arise and come forth unto me, that ye may thrust your hands into my side, and also that ye may feel the prints of the nails in my hands and in my feet, that ye may know that I am the God of Israel, and the God of the whole earth, and have been slain for the sins of the world.' "

He invited them to come up one by one. They touched the wounds in his hands and the prints of the nails in his feet. And when they had all gone forth, they cried out and fell down at his feet and worshipped him.

The deeper I went, the more I loved him.

A few days later I was ready to be baptized.

"What do you think about the church?" I cautiously asked Jim.

"It's all right, I guess," he mumbled.

"Well, you like the missionaries, don't you?"

"Yeah, I guess so."

"And you liked Cub Scout day camp, right?"

"It was okay," he said.

"Then c'mon, let's both get baptized the same day. Afterwards Kellie's invited us over to her house for some cake and ice cream."

He shook his head. "Dad, you'd better go ahead without me."

I sat down beside him and put my arm around him. "What's wrong?"

"If we become Mormons, then maybe that'll make Mom mad, and she won't ever come back to us."

I sighed. "Jim, she's not coming back."

"She might. She might decide she loves us and come back again. We should be ready in case she does."

"The reason she left was because of me, not you. She still loves you. It's just that she and I don't get along. I can see now that a lot of it was my fault. But it's too late for her and me. She's not coming back. I know that's hard to hear, but you've just got to accept it."

"But people change their minds sometimes, don't they?" he asked.

*   *   *   *   *

Ben and his wife invited Kellie and me and our kids over on a Monday night.

It was interesting to see Ben as a father. The man who was always racing off to a meeting—at home he was just another dad. When we arrived at their house, he was outside fixing his boy's bike.

We met his wife, Vicky, an attractive, lively woman with four kids. We had an outdoor barbecue, and afterwards their kids put on a program. The oldest took charge and introduced the rest. Ben sat and watched and smiled proudly and, at the same time, turned the ice-cream maker.

A little later that night, while Kellie and Vicky put the dishes into the dishwasher, I had a chance to talk to Ben about Jim not wanting to join the church.

"Don't force him," he said. "Let him come to the decision by himself."

"I'm not sure I can wait that long," I said. "I'm ready now."

"Then I think you should go ahead and be baptized. Jim will follow when he's ready."

*   *   *   *   *

The next time the missionaries came, I told them I wanted to be baptized. We set the date, and they made arrangements for me to be interviewed for baptism. Just before they left, they asked if I knew of anybody else who would benefit from the church.

"Well, my mom and my sister would." They suggested I phone and tell them about my joining and ask if they'd like to learn more about it.

So later that night I phoned Kalispell, Montana. "Beth, this is Michael."

There was a long pause at her end.

"You know, your brother Michael?"

"I know who you are," she snapped. "Are you calling to try and borrow some money? Look, we don't have any. We're barely making it ourselves."

"Nothing like that. I want you to know that I'm being baptized this weekend into the Mormon church."

A long silence, and then, "Sure, it figures. I guess you know they're not Christian, don't you?"

"Beth, it's called The Church of Jesus Christ of Latter-day Saints. How can they not be Christian?"

"Have they told you about their gold bible?"

"I've read it. You ought to read it too, Beth. Especially if you love Jesus."

"I've got enough to do just keeping up with my church."

She was through discussing religion.

"I'm filing for divorce next month."

"Have you told Wally yet?"

"Not yet."

"Do the kids know?"

"No. That's the part I dread. But it'll be better this way."

"Can I send you any money for the kids?"

"Do you have a steady job yet?"

"I'm working on a movie. We think it's going to do real well."

She'd heard that before. "Is this a sequel to *Hog Butcher?*"

Next I phoned my mother in Arizona and told her about it.

"That's nice, dear."

"Would you like to know about it too, Mom?"

"No, I don't think so, but you go ahead."

"Mom, I'm dating someone now. She's been married before. She's a Mormon. Her husband died in a car accident about a year ago."

"Do you think you'll marry her?"

"It's too early to tell, but I'll keep you posted."

*   *   *   *   *

There was prelude music before the service began. I sat on the first row wearing white baptismal clothes.

I thought about the movie, and how hard it had been to try to be like the Savior for even ten minutes at a time when all I had to do was to repeat the lines I'd memorized.

And now I was about to take upon me his name.

He asked the question once of his disciples, "What manner of men ought ye to be?" His answer was, "Even as I am."

Impossible? Of course. But worth the effort to try.

I was back to being an understudy, but this time it would never end with the closing of a play.

The service began. Ben baptized me, confirmed me, and then ordained me a priest.

Afterwards we went to Kellie's and had cake and ice cream. Jim was very quiet that night.

CHAPTER TEN

We finished the movie in October.

I stayed in Utah to be with Kellie. Because my salary from the movie had stopped and the deferred payments would come only after the movie opened in theaters, I was a little low on funds. To tide me over, I got a job at a car wash.

Suddenly I was counting my wealth in the number of times I could get her to smile, or when she'd call up and ask me to come fix something around her house, or when after a date, we'd stand at the door and embrace. She still didn't want to kiss me, but she let me hold her in my arms.

It was a stormy time, though, for both of us. Her moods swung erratically from one extreme to the other. Sometimes she clung to me for support. At other times she'd lash out as if she were trying to destroy everything between us. And it always ended with her saying that maybe we shouldn't see each other anymore.

One night I showed up for a date and she said, "Are you ever going to shave off that beard?"

"I like it."

"Do you know what I think about a man who wears a beard? I think he's hiding something. You don't want people to see the real you, so you put this bush over your face." She went into the bathroom and brought out Steve's razor and handed it to me. "I'm not going out with you again until you shave it off."

It was an ultimatum. She'd given it because she didn't really think I'd do it.

And so I did.

Half an hour later I came out clean-shaven. She took one look at me and said, "I guess I liked you better with the beard."

I was so mad I couldn't even talk. I walked out on her.

A day later when I got home from work, she was sitting on my doorstep. "I came to apologize. I'm sorry for being so rotten. I don't know why I'm so mean sometimes. Actually I think you're very handsome with or without a beard."

Of course we didn't spend every minute together. We each still had meals to cook, clothes to wash, and houses to clean up.

"I've really had it with Jim," I said one night on the phone.

"What's wrong?"

"I fix a nice meal, turkey and mashed potatoes. Jim sits down and scarfs it down in about three seconds and then he just walks away. Not a word of thanks. I mean, what good does it do to knock myself out? Why couldn't he at least tell me he liked it?"

"He probably just forgot," she said.

"It was as good as anything Pamela ever cooked," I grumbled.

"I'm sure it was."

"Except for the gravy," I admitted. "I have a little trouble with gravy."

"Well, maybe I can help. This is the way I do gravy . . ."

I was taking notes as she talked. And then I burst out laughing. "What am I coming to? I'm starting to sound like Harriet Homemaker! This is ridiculous. Before you know it, I'll be making little doilies."

"Hey, what about me? I can walk into a hardware store now and ask for a molly bolt without batting an eye."

"This single parenthood is really getting me down. How about you?"

"I agree. Sometimes I feel so alone, like it's me against the entire world."

"Hey, I've got an idea. How about if we get married?"

She laughed. "Oh, sure, you're just looking for a way out of having to learn to make gravy."

I laughed too, but deep inside I wished she hadn't tossed the idea off so quickly.

*   *   *   *   *

Once she phoned me at twelve-thirty at night. "I can't get to sleep tonight. I need someone to talk to."

"We can talk on the phone if you want."

"Since midnight it's been one year since Steve died."

She told me everything about the day he died. How cheerful he'd been in the morning, how they'd talked about how they were going to meet their bills, about an exam he was going to have that day, and about whether or not they'd be able to go to the next football game.

And then it had all ended so quickly.

"Why did he have to go and die?" she said miserably.

She cried for a long time.

* * * * *

The next time I asked her out she said, "I'm sorry but I already have a date that night."

"What?"

"I think we've been spending too much time together. You should date others too."

"Who are you going out with?"

"I don't think that's any business of yours."

"I want to know. Who is he?"

"He's in law school at the Y. We used to know each other in high school."

I spent the day of her date fixing my car, giving it a tune-up to keep it going a few more miles. If I could just wait until the movie opened, I'd start getting some money and then I'd buy myself a Corvette. No woman was going to stop me from getting the car of my dreams. Women aren't worth it.

At nine that night Kellie came over to my house.

"Your date's over already?" I asked.

She sighed. "It was terrible. First of all, when he showed up at my door, he was wearing enough after-shave to be a fire hazard.

"When I introduced him to Rusty, he asked how old he was, and Rusty told him eight, and he said from Rusty's size he would've guessed maybe five or six. What a stupid thing to say to a boy.

"And then we went out in his car and he had a tape deck and

it was playing soft music—and he draped his arm over the seat. It was like his arm was some vulture just waiting for the right time to pounce on my shoulders.

"But his biggest mistake was when he asked me what was wrong with Rusty. I got mad and asked him what was wrong with his heart. I really told him off and then demanded he take me home. When I got inside the house again, I started to cry. Rusty told me I'd better go see you because you always make me feel better, and so here I am. I'm such a basket case, will you let me stay for a while?"

"Sure, but you might as well know that I'm broke. I spent all my money today on a carburetor kit."

"I don't care," she said. "Just let me hang around here with you, okay?"

We went into the kitchen and had graham crackers and milk. I dunked mine. She didn't.

"Steve liked graham crackers too," she said.

"He and I like a lot of the same things. Graham crackers and you."

"How much did it cost for parts to fix up your car?" she asked.

"About thirty dollars, but if I'd had a garage do it, it would have cost at least a hundred." I reached out and held her hand. "It seems natural to be here like this, doesn't it, just the two of us, talking things over in the kitchen."

She could see what was coming. "I haven't thought about it before."

"But you know I love you, don't you?"

She looked away. "Yes, I guess I do."

"Do you love me?"

She didn't answer.

"Well, I'd better put the milk away," I said abruptly, standing up. "One day last week Jim left a carton out all night. We had to throw it away. Nearly a full half gallon too. And then he wonders why I can't afford to buy him video games."

"Michael, let me explain."

"You don't need to explain. It's all right, really it is. I was out of place to even ask. Do you want any more milk before I put it away?''

"Just forget the milk, okay? Look, let me be honest with you. I'm just not sure how I feel about you, except that I know I need you. Sometimes I feel like I'm drowning and you're the only life raft in my ocean.''

I paused. "You need me?''

"Absolutely. All the time.''

"That's good. Maybe we should go into the living room.''

She was puzzled. "Why the living room?''

"I have a big favor to ask you, and I'm afraid to ask it here in the kitchen.''

"What's wrong with the kitchen?''

"We need a place that's kind of romantic.''

"What do you want to talk about?''

"I have a big favor to ask.''

"What is it?''

"Hold on a minute, okay?''

I rummaged through a cupboard until I found a candle. I lit it and used the drippings to stick it upright on the kitchen table. Then I turned on the radio and found a station playing mood music. I excused myself, hurried into the bathroom, and splashed after-shave on my face and neck, then I remembered what she'd said about her date's after-shave, so I washed it all off again, and then returned and turned off the light so we were bathed in candlelight. I sat down next to her.

I waited through one romantic song and then said, "Kellie, I want you to quit wearing Steve's wedding ring.''

"Why?''

"I want you to wear mine. I'm asking you to marry me.''

She sighed. "I knew this was coming. Michael, it's too soon. I'm still not over losing Steve.''

"I'm not asking you to stop loving him. Just give me a small place in your heart. An upstairs attic, a closet, a storeroom, there must be some place left. That's all I ask.''

"I've been through too much to start over as a blushing bride.''

I smiled. "It's all right with me if you don't blush."

She fought back a smile. "You know what I mean."

"Sure, but look, we won't be starting out from scratch. We'll have two kids right off the bat."

"Steve and I shared some intimate memories. I'm not sure I want to repeat them with anyone else."

"Did he propose to you in candlelight after you'd both had graham crackers and milk?"

"No."

"See there? The memories won't be the same."

"I'm just not sure I want to go changing horses in the middle of the stream."

"Don't think of it like you're in the middle of the stream. Think of it like you're still in the corral. At first you choose this one horse called Single Mother, but then you see another called Remarried. You ask the man in charge if it'd be all right to change your mind, and he says, 'Go ahead.' So he saddles up the other horse for you. So you see, it's not in the middle of the stream—you're still in the corral."

She laughed. "Do graham crackers always do this to you?"

The mood music stopped. The announcer was introducing a farm specialist who was going to answer questions about the application of fungicides. I switched to another station.

"I think we're ready for the living room now, don't you?" I asked.

I carried the candle in and we sat down on the sofa, which had a horse blanket on it to hide the rip in the cushions. With only a candle for light, it was dark enough to hide the fact that Jim's sneakers and dirty socks were still on the floor where he'd left them that night. It was almost dark enough in the room to be romantic.

I reached out and held her hand. "I think we've gone as far as we can as friends. It's time to move on. I want to be the one you ask to fasten the top button in the back of your Sunday dress when you're getting ready for church. And the one to keep you toasty warm when you're sleeping during those long winter nights." I paused. "Unless we're married, we won't be able to share those experiences together. So why not get married?"

"You realize, don't you, that I can't be your wife after we die."

"Right now I'm worried about getting through next week. I lie awake every night thinking about you. I need my sleep. Besides, there's something you should know about me."

"What?"

"When I was a senior in high school, I was the second-string quarterback for the football team. I didn't play until the final game of our season. In the second half our star quarterback sprained his ankle. There was nobody else available, so the coach had to send me in. I played the entire second half."

"Did your team win?"

"Kellie," I grumbled, "that's not the point"

There was just the glimmer of a smile on her face. "I'm sorry. What's the point?"

"The point is that I've spent a lot of my life in the shadows of better men, sort of filling in for them. Now that Steve's gone, let me do that for you too. I love you and I want you to be my wife."

She sighed. "You really do, don't you."

"Very much. A few weeks from now I want us to be sitting here like this, and you'll yawn, and I'll put out the cat, and just before we go to bed, we'll look in on our boys to make sure they've got their covers on, and everything will be okay, and we won't have to say goodbye at the end of the day anymore."

She got up from the sofa and walked to the window and looked out.

A long time passed and then she turned around. I could just barely see her face in the candlelight. "We don't have a cat."

"We'll get a cat."

"I don't want a cat."

"Me either."

A full minute passed before she said with a sigh, "All right, I accept."

"You mean it?"

"Yes."

"That means we're engaged, doesn't it?"

"Yes, it does."

"May I kiss you?"

She sighed. "I guess there's no reason not to now, is there?"

"I guess not. It'll be our first time."

"I know, but it's all right."

On my way to her on the other side of the room, I tripped on Jim's shoe and twisted my ankle and fell down.

"Are you all right?" she asked.

"No problem!" I cheerfully assured her, getting back up. "It was nothing, really." I hobbled over and kissed her for the first time.

My ankle was killing me. I suggested we sit down on the couch.

After we'd kissed a few times, she tensed up, as if a part of her felt it wasn't right to be kissing me. At my suggestion, we returned to the kitchen and ate graham crackers and made plans.

Although I was glad she'd agreed to marry me, I was a little disappointed she wasn't more excited about it.

                    *   *   *   *   *

The next day she phoned to tell her parents she was going to marry a divorced movie actor who worked at a car wash. They rushed down from Idaho to rescue her.

"You're not as large a man as I pictured," her father told me right after we'd met.

"Why's that?"

"Kellie said you were an actor and that you once played the part of a hog butcher. I just figured you'd be a big man."

"The movie was about Carl Sandburg. He wrote a poem once describing Chicago as the hog butcher of the world."

"Oh. Look, we might as well be honest with each other. I don't like the thought of my daughter marrying someone who's already failed at marriage."

"Daddy," Kellie said, "his first wife left him with their son just because she wanted a career. It wasn't Michael's fault."

"Is that true?" her father asked.

"That's what I told Kellie when I first met her. But now I can see that a good part of it was my fault."

"Can you guarantee a second marriage won't end in divorce too?"

"No, but I do know I've changed since I've come down here. I've played the part of Jesus in a movie, and that's changed me a lot. And I've joined the Mormon church. I promise to try and be the kind of husband Kellie needs. I love her with all my heart."

Kellie looked at her father. "Daddy, he's good to Rusty, and he's considerate of me. I really think it'd be better for all of us if he and I get married."

"Well, if you really think so, I guess that's what you should do then."

She didn't tell her parents that she loved me.

*   *   *   *   *

We were married in November in the Relief Society room at church, with Jim and Rusty standing alongside us during the ceremony. They were our best men, but we jokingly called them our best boys.

Mom had flown in from Arizona for the wedding. She looked good. She'd taken the money from the sale on the house and some savings and had used it on herself. I think it was the first time in her life she'd ever bought anything just because she wanted it. She was just about to go on a package tour to Hawaii. She and Kellie got along well.

There were all sorts of introductions to be made in the reception line that day.

"Michael," Kellie said during the reception, "I'd like you to meet Steve's parents."

"Hi there. Nice to meet you."

"I hope you know what a wonderful girl you're getting," Steve's mother said.

"Oh, yes, I sure do."

"Steve was so happy with Kellie," Steve's father said.

"I'm sure I will be too."

"And this is Steve's younger brother Alan."

"Alan, nice to meet you."

Alan, seventeen years old, was fiercely loyal to Steve. "Steve'll have her after she dies."

Maybe so, I thought with an inward smile, but I have her now. But I didn't say that. "Alan, I know you think that Steve and I are rivals, but I think Steve approves of this, because he loves Kellie and wants her to be as happy as she can now."

Kellie squeezed my hand. It was the right thing to say.

*   *   *   *   *

We stayed in the Hotel Utah our first night together.

When I came out of the bathroom in my pajamas, she was standing at the window wearing a lace nightgown, looking out at the temple across the street.

I was very nervous. "I think it was nice of them to give us shampoo, don't you? I mean, how many hotels give a little packet of free shampoo?"

She turned to look at me, and that made me even more nervous.

"The only trouble was, I couldn't get it open. Finally I used my teeth to rip it open, but that caused some shampoo to squirt into my mouth." I paused awkwardly. "Uh, so if I start frothing at the mouth later tonight, you'll know . . ."

I stopped talking.

She smiled at me. "Let me guess. You're a little nervous?"

I paused. "Actually a lot."

"Me too. Come over and let's look out at the temple."

We stood, arm in arm, looking at the temple I'd never been in.

"Were you and Steve ever inside the Salt Lake Temple?"

"Yes, several times."

"And the Hotel Utah?"

"We ate at the rooftop restaurant once."

"It gets kind of crowded around here sometimes, doesn't it?"

She nodded her head.

I kissed her. For just a second it was very nice, and then she tensed up again and broke away. "I think we should call Jim and Rusty to see how they're doing."

We made the call. Her parents were staying with them that

night. We talked to our boys. And then we said goodnight and hung up.

It was a little awkward. We both looked warily at each other.

I smiled. "I've got an idea. The hotel's given us a bunch of free postcards. How about us sending them to all the kids in our high school graduation classes. And when we get done with that, we'll see if the registration desk'll loan us a deck of cards. Let me guess—I'll bet you're good at playing Old Maid, right?"

She smiled and grabbed my hand. "I've got a better idea."

"What's that?"

"Let's just say our prayers and go to bed."

*   *   *   *   *

A week later she came to me looking worried. "There's something I need to tell you. It's been on my mind since I woke up this morning."

"What is it?"

"I had a dream last night about Steve. He showed up here and said it had all been a mistake, that he hadn't really died after all. He asked me to go with him." She paused. "Michael, in my dream I left you and went with him."

"This was a dream?" I asked.

"Yes."

"Don't worry about it. We can't control our dreams. It's just going to take some time to sort everything out."

She felt so guilty she wouldn't even look at me. "But if he did come back, I'd go with him even though I'm married to you. I'd leave you if he came back."

"Kellie," I said softly, "he's not coming back. So I don't think it's something we need to worry very much about, okay?"

She gave a sigh of relief. "Okay."

"Don't worry about night dreams," I said. "But what about daydreams? Do you ever daydream about Steve?"

"Sometimes," she reluctantly admitted. "Even our first night together, after you'd fallen asleep, I lay awake and thought about him."

Now I couldn't look at her. "Did you think about your honeymoon with him?"

"Yes," she said softly.

I was devastated. All along I'd thought that after we got married I'd be able to give her so much love she'd forget about Steve. For the first time I had to face that I might always come in a poor second to him.

I didn't tell her how bad I felt. "Why shouldn't you think about him? You've got a lot of good memories with him. But listen to me, I'm going to give you some terrific memories too."

I'd taken away her guilt, and she gratefully melted into my arms. "Oh, Michael, you're so good to me. I love you more each day."

Beautiful Lady, I thought, that's what I'm counting on.

CHAPTER ELEVEN

Soon after we returned from our honeymoon, I insisted we see about selling her house because of all the memories she had of Steve there. But after visiting with a real estate agent, I realized we'd be better off financially just to stay put.

There were times those first few weeks when I thought that maybe Kellie had been right, maybe it had been too soon for her to get married again. The problem was Steve. He was never very far from us.

For instance, she came to me with a simple suggestion of how to arrange my side of the closet. "How about having your shirts on the left on wire hangers, and your slacks and suits on the right on wooden hangers. What would you think of that?"

"Is that the way Steve did it?"

"Yes, it is."

"I thought so."

"Don't just toss it aside because of that. It worked out very well."

"For Steve maybe, but I do things my own way. And I'd appreciate it if you'd quit trying to make me into his clone. It's bad enough that I have to sleep on his pillow at night. Now you even want me to hang my clothes up the way he did."

"Do it any way you want then. I'm through giving suggestions to you." She tossed me an angry glare and went into the kitchen.

I stayed in the bedroom and fumed. I was about to go tell her I was sick and tired of hearing Steve this and Steve that. She was my wife now, and she'd better start acting like it. Besides, if Steve was so perfect, like everybody says, why did he let himself fall asleep at the wheel? Anybody knows that if you get sleepy when you're driving, you should pull over and take a nap.

While I crammed my clothes in the closet, purposely making a mess just to teach her a lesson, a shirt fell on the floor. I reached down to pick it up. In a box on the floor I saw my script for the movie about Jesus. I started thumbing through it. My lines, the things that Jesus said, were underlined in red.

The phrase, *What manner of men ought ye to be,* rang through my mind.

Jesus again.

A few minutes later I'd cooled down enough to go talk to her. "I'm sorry for snapping at you."

"No, it was my fault. I had no business telling you how to do your closet."

"I don't care about the closet. I just need to know that you love me."

"You know I do."

"Do you love me more than Steve?"

"Michael, that's not fair."

I sighed. "I guess not."

"I love you more each day."

She said that a lot to me at first. I was never sure if it meant she hadn't loved me very much when we'd gotten married, or if it was just a way to avoid having to tell me she'd never love me as much as she did Steve.

But what if it was true? If she loved me more each day, maybe she'd end up loving me more than she did him. And if she did, maybe in the hereafter she'd choose me. At least it was a possibility.

*   *   *   *   *

One Sunday afternoon after church, Kellie and I lay down for a nap. The boys were next door playing with friends. When I woke up, the sun was shining through the bedroom window, showing dust patterns dancing in the sun. The sunlight caused the copper-colored strands in her hair to come alive. Her face was calm in sleep and full of beauty. There I was, her husband, lying next to her, the luckiest man in the world.

The sun reached her eyes, and she awoke and looked at me and realized I'd been watching her sleep. She smiled and held out her arms and welcomed me even closer.

I loved being near her. Sometimes I tried to tell her what it was like for me to be a part of the beauty and goodness I saw in her, but I don't think she ever really understood what I meant.

I know that it made me want to be better.

*   *   *   *   *

Not long after we were married, I had an offer to star in a major Hollywood movie about a mass murderer who'd killed forty-seven women.

"Why did you think of me for the part?" I asked the producer who had phoned me.

"Because you have a face that's easy to trust. That's the way he was. Women trusted him. That's why he got to so many."

"I can't do that."

"Why not?"

"I've just finished a movie where I played the part of Jesus."

"So what? You're an actor. You play the parts that come along. Each one presents a different challenge. We all have good and evil in us. You've played from the good side—now make use of your dark side."

"I can't do a mass murderer."

"What are you going to do," he sneered, "play nice guys from now on?"

I paused. "I know you won't understand this, but once you've played the role of Jesus, you're never the same again."

"Quit acting then and get a job selling shoes if that's the way you feel. Look, think it over. This movie'll make you a rich man."

I talked to Kellie. She knew how much we needed the money. She said she'd understand if I took the part.

A day later I reached a decision. "I'm afraid to do it. What if some of that character rubbed off on me, what if I started looking at women the way he did? No, I can't do it. Besides I can't leave you now."

"Why not?"

"I'd miss you too much."

I turned down the role. The producer was right. The movie made a lot of money. But money isn't everything.

*   *   *   *   *

Things seemed to be going fine with us until one Saturday. We were at the breakfast table, and Kellie, still in her robe, put an egg on Jim's plate.

"I'm not going to eat that," he grumbled.

"Why not?"

"It's runny. I hate runny eggs."

"No problem," Kellie said good-naturedly. "I'll cook it a little more."

She scooped up the egg and put it back in the frying pan until it was well done. Then she set it back on Jim's plate.

"Not that way," he griped. "Now it's too hard."

"Eat it anyway," I snapped.

"No."

"That's all right," Kellie said, trying to smooth things over. "I'll eat that one. Jim, would you rather have it scrambled?"

"I just want it the way my Mom fixed it."

"How was that?"

"Forget it, okay? You'll never learn how."

"Just tell me how you want it and I'll try."

"I don't want anything from you. Just leave me alone."

"Don't talk to your mother that way," I scolded.

"She's not my mother!" He got up and ran outside.

I told Kellie it wasn't her fault, and then I went out after Jim. I found him in the garage sitting in the driver's seat of the car. I sat down beside him in the car.

"Dad, why'd you have to wreck everything by getting married again? Now Mom'll never come back to us."

"She never would have come back anyway. I know this is hard on you, but the four of us are a family now, and I need you to try to make this thing work out. You've got a new mom, and a brother too."

"He's not my brother," he scoffed. "What a dumbhead. Last night he forgot where he put his glasses and bumped his head on the door on his way to the bathroom."

"That's not his fault."

"If you ask me, we were better off up at the lake. At least we didn't have them to worry about."

"I want you to go back and apologize to Kellie. She's really trying to be a good mom to you. Can't you meet her half way?"

He paused. "Okay, but I won't eat her dumb eggs."

We went back inside and he halfheartedly apologized. I thought it was over, but that Sunday morning, before church, we had more problems. Rusty had taken a shower, and now it was twenty minutes before church started. He came out of the bathroom with just a towel wrapped around him. "I can't find my glasses."

"Where did you leave them?" Kellie asked.

"On the counter in the bathroom."

"We're going to be late," Kellie said. She went in the bathroom and looked. They weren't there.

We looked all over.

Then I saw Jim outside on the swings with a smirk on his face. I opened the back door. "All right! Where did you put them?"

"Put what?"

"You know what I mean. Where did you put Rusty's glasses?"

He smirked. "In the tree. If he wants them, let him climb it, if he can."

I went over and grabbed his arm and yanked him out of the swing. "You go get them right now!"

He climbed the tree and got the glasses and came down and handed them to me.

"Now get ready for church. We're already going to be late."

"I'm not going," he said.

"You are too."

"It's not my church. It's her church. I'm staying home like we always did before we came to Utah."

"Listen to me. While you're in this house, you'll do what I say."

"You can't make me go to church if I don't want to. It's not my church."

"All right, what church do you want to go to?"

He looked surprised. "What?"

"You're going to church this morning, so tell me what church it is you want me to drop you off at."

"You're just going to leave me at some church I've never been to before?"

"That's right. Now go in, and while you're getting dressed, you decide what church you want, Methodist, Catholic, Baptist, whatever you decide."

He went inside.

Fifteen minutes later we got in the car and started out the driveway.

"Have you decided where you want me to take you?" I asked him.

He paused. "I guess I'll just go with you today," he muttered.

*   *   *   *   *

One day several weeks later, the principal asked me to come to the school. He said Jim was in trouble.

When I arrived, I was told that Jim had been fighting in school. I asked Jim why, and he said some boys were picking on Rusty.

"At first I didn't care if they hurt him or not, but then a boy hit Rusty in the stomach and started laughing about it. I didn't think that was fair, so I told him to lay off, and he told me to stay out of it, and I said, why don't you pick on somebody your own size, and he tried to hit me, and that got me mad. And so I hit him in the stomach the way he'd hit Rusty, and then some of his friends tried to gang up on us."

The principal said that when a teacher finally came to see what the noise was about, he found Jim and Rusty, back to back, protecting each other, waiting to see if anyone else was going to take them on.

"We can't have fighting in the school," the principal said.

"Then I'd suggest you talk to the boys who started it. My boys don't fight unless they're attacked."

Jim nodded. "And you tell 'em, if they start anything with Rusty, they'll have to fight me too."

The principal tried to make me feel bad that Jim cared enough about his stepbrother to protect him, but it didn't work.

Just before we got home, I told the boys I didn't want them fighting in school, but that I was proud of them for sticking together.

* * * * *

We still had Moby Dick. It seemed that every time we'd finally get enough money to get something better, the washing machine would break down or the water heater would go out, and we'd end up using the money for that instead of a better car.

One Saturday I showed the boys how to do a tune-up. They hung around on the hood and watched me, much as I'd done around my own dad. When we came in, the boys were still excited about learning how to fix cars.

Kellie smiled at me. "You're becoming quite the dad these days, you know that?"

I smiled. "I was hoping you'd notice."

* * * * *

After the next stake conference I was ordained an elder in the church. A few nights later Kellie asked me to give a father's blessing to Rusty because he had a bad cough.

"I'm not sure what to do."

"If you want, I can tell you how Steve did it." Then she caught herself and looked at me to see if that was going to make me mad.

I smiled. "Yes, I'd like to know."

She explained the details, finally ending with, "Just listen to the Spirit."

I felt inadequate. What if the Spirit didn't tell me anything? "Kellie, maybe we'd better call our home teachers."

"No, you're his father now. I want you to do it."

"I'm not Steve."

She came over and touched my face. "I love you very much. I know that you and God will be able to work out a priesthood blessing. Please, Michael."

I nodded. "Give me a few minutes, okay?"

I went into our bedroom and prayed. A few minutes later I returned. "I'm ready now."

After the blessing, she hugged me and said it was just right.

Jim, who'd watched the whole thing, said no when I asked if he wanted a father's blessing too.

*   *   *   *   *

It began with a phone call in the early summer of the next year.

I was outside putting our camping gear into the trunk of the car. Rusty and Jim and I were going up to Strawberry Reservoir to be there for the opening day of fishing season.

"Hey, guys, look what I got." I showed them three packages of frozen strawberries and two jars of roasted peanuts. "Okay now, when your friends ask you what we lived on while we were camping, you tell 'em we survived on berries and nuts, okay?"

"The phone's for you," Kellie called out from the house.

"You guys finish packing, and I'll be right back."

I walked inside. "It's a woman," Kellie said.

I picked up the phone and said hello.

It was long distance. "Michael, is that you? This is Pamela."

"Pamela, hello."

"Did you hear about me getting married again?" she asked.

"No, I didn't, Pamela."

"It was three weeks ago. We just got back from our honeymoon. We went to Bermuda. It was wonderful there."

"I got married too, Pamela."

"I know. Jimmy wrote and told me about it." She paused. "He didn't sound very happy about it."

"It'll work out. It will just take some time. Who did you marry?"

"A surgeon. I met him at the hospital where I was working. His name is Whittaker Alceister."

"Sounds like a good name for *you*, Pamela."

"Now that I can afford to travel, we'd like to come out and see Jimmy."

I was secretly glad she was still calling him Jimmy.

"Gosh, I hate to have you go to that much trouble. How about if I just send you some snapshots?"

"Whittaker has a conference in Utah. We're flying out next week. We'll be there next Friday. We'd like to spend a few days with Jimmy."

"Gosh, ordinarily that'd be fine, but we're planning a camping trip then."

"Michael, don't play games with me. I have the right to see my own son, don't I?"

I sighed. "All right. Next Friday, you say? How long do you want to *see* him?"

"Three days," she said. "We'll have him back on Monday night."

A week later they came in a rented Lincoln Continental. Whittaker was what you would expect from a brain surgeon. Polished, bright, witty, handsome, rich, and smart. Pamela looked good in the clothes he could afford for her.

Whittaker and I verbally dueled out in the driveway while we waited for Pamela and Kellie to quit talking.

"Pamela tells me you're sort of an actor."

"That's right."

"Would I have seen you in anything?"

"Are you a fan of Carl Sandburg?"

"Not really."

"Then I doubt if you've seen me. But then again, I doubt I've met any brains you've sawed into either."

We both chuckled pleasantly.

He looked at Moby *Dick* parked in the driveway. "Does that

actually run, or is it just being stored until someone has time to haul it to the junkyard?"

"It runs fine."

He paused. "Well, tell me what movie you're working on now."

I paused. "I'm between movies."

"What does that mean?"

"It means I did a movie, and now I'm waiting to do another one."

"Oh, I see. You're out of work. Well, I guess that explains the car then, doesn't it?"

"What are you and Pamela planning on doing with Jimmy this weekend?" I asked. I hoped they'd call him Jimmy all the time they were with him.

"Well, knowing boys, I thought first we'd take him to a video arcade, and then I've arranged for him to have his first flying lesson." He paused and then smiled faintly. "Also, we thought it'd be fun for us all to learn how to windsurf."

"I'm not sure if it's warm enough for that yet."

"We were thinking more of California. We're going there tomorrow anyway to see Disneyland."

I scowled. "Oh."

Jim came out with his mother and made a fool of himself drooling over their car. Whittaker promised to let him drive.

When they left, Jim didn't even wave goodbye to me.

That night, from the way I was tossing and turning, it was obvious I couldn't get to sleep.

Kellie turned on the light. "Do you want to talk about it?"

"They're going to take him away from me. I know they are."

"They said it was just for a few days."

"You don't know Pamela like I do. She's devious, and now she's got Whittaker to pay the bills."

When Jim returned from the weekend, all he could talk about was how neat Whittaker was, and how much money they'd spent, and how they'd let him do anything he wanted.

I offered to go out and buy him and Rusy an ice cream cone, but he said he was sick of ice cream. He'd had too much of it in California.

"What did they ask about us?" I asked.

"They wanted to know if I ever went to bed hungry."

"What did you tell them?"

"I told them that sometimes I did."

"Are you crazy? Why did you say that? We're feeding you three good meals a day, aren't we?"

"Sometimes I want a snack before I go to bed, and you tell me it's too late."

"Look, if anybody ever asks you again, you tell them you get good nourishing meals. What else did they ask you?"

"They asked where you bought my clothes. I told them about how Kellie goes to garage sales and buys us old clothes that nobody else wants."

"Oh yeah? Well, what about that pair of jeans we bought you in Sears last month?"

"That was my birthday present. I told them about that."

"What else did they want to know?"

"If you have a job."

"What did you tell them?"

"That you work in a car wash."

"What did they say?"

"Whittaker said that the next time they came to see me, maybe he'd go by while you're working and have you wash his car."

"What else did they say?"

"They told me a lot about Boston and asked if I'd ever like to come out and see it."

"Listen to me," I warned. "People in Boston have to eat codfish and baked beans every day."

He looked worried.

"Tell me, does Whittaker drink?"

"A little. He had some wine after dinner one night."

"Did he ever get drunk while you were there?"

"No."

"There's a lot of stress on a man like him. He's probably on his way to becoming an alcoholic, just like your uncle Wally."

"Stress?"

"That means he worries a lot."

"Why should he worry? He's got money. I think Kellie worries the most of anybody. You hardly give her anything to buy food with."

"We get by, don't we? And another thing—I'd like you to start calling her Mom."

"She's not my mom."

"I know that, but is it going to kill you to call her Mom?"

"Then I'd have two moms. Besides, Kellie said it's okay if I call her Kellie."

"What else did they talk about?"

"Mom asked if I knew there was a clause in the divorce agreement that anytime she wanted, she could request a hearing to get me back again."

My mouth dropped open. "What?"

I'd never looked at the divorce papers. All I'd done was sign them.

*   *   *   *   *

A month passed and nothing happened. I started to relax and think maybe I'd just imagined Pamela was out to get custody of Jim. Kellie and I kept waiting for him to say he wanted to be baptized, but he still seemed reluctant.

Our first big check from the deferred payments for the movie finally arrived. We spent several days shopping and finally picked out a used station wagon in good condition. We'd be able to put down over half the money for the car and handle the rest with monthly payments.

And then it happened. I got an official-looking letter from California announcing a reconvening of the court to determine my suitability as a parent.

Our extra money went to hire an attorney in California, where the hearing would be held. Our lawyer was just out of law school. He had long hair and wore a turtleneck sweater and corduroy slacks.

Their lawyer wore a suit with a vest and had gray hair.

"Mr. Hill, can you tell us what your present employment is?" their attorney began.

"Well, right now I'm between movies."

"Are you saying you are presently unemployed?"

"No, I work part time at a car wash."

"In what capacity?"

"Finishing," I said.

"Could you tell us exactly what you do?"

"As a car goes by, I wipe off excess water on the left-hand side and the front bumper. The other guys get the rest."

"How much does that pay?"

"Two ninety-five per hour, but I'm due a raise next month."

"How much does that bring in during the course of a month?"

"Well, during an average month, maybe about five hundred dollars."

"Do you find that adequate to run a family of four on?"

"No, but I have other income, of course. For instance, on the movie I did about Carl Sandburg I made twenty thousand dollars."

"I see. Well, let's go into that. Over the past ten years, can you tell us how much you've made from acting?"

I paused. "I don't have all the figures right here at my disposal."

"Just an estimate. Take your time. We'll wait."

I took a pencil and figured. A minute later I looked up. "About fifty thousand dollars."

"In ten years? Let's see, that's about five thousand dollars a year, isn't it?"

"Hey, since when does a man's value as a father depend on how much he makes? My son and I do things together. That's worth a lot."

Pamela's attorney played a phone-recorded statement from Beth. She talked about visiting us at the lake right after my divorce. "Jimmy begged me to let him come to my house and live," she'd said.

"I see," the lawyer had replied. "What exactly was inadequate about the way Mr. Hill was providing for his son?"

"Well, for one thing, he made Jimmy drink coffee because he said he couldn't afford milk. And while they were there, the water pump went out and they had to drink lake water. I wouldn't be surprised but that there's raw sewage going into that lake. It's a wonder they didn't come down with something.''

"Did Mr. Hill have any kind of a job while he was there at the lake?''

"No. I offered to have him come and work for my husband. But holding down a job is something my brother just can't seem to manage. If you ask me, he's just plain lazy. I've always said that about him."

And then she started in about me joining a non-Christian cult.

I'd had enough by then. "I'd like to answer that," I said.

They stopped the tape, and the judge let me talk. I told them how I'd changed because of the movie, and how that in everything I did now, I tried to let Jesus be my example.

Next Pamela's attorney asked permission to talk to Jim.

"What do you think of the Mormon church?''

Jim shrugged. "It's all right, I guess.''

"Is there anything that bothers you about it?''

He paused. "Well, the main thing I don't like about it is Sundays. We go to church at nine and we don't get out until noon."

"You think that's too long?''

"Sure, don't you?''

"Is there anything else you don't like about that church?''

"I don't like singing time in Primary.''

"Why not?''

"Because I don't like singing songs about blossoms on apricot trees, like they're supposed to look like popcorn. To me blossoms are one thing and popcorn is another. I never get the two mixed up."

The attorney decided to change the subject. "If you could change anything about your father, what would it be?''

Our lawyer objected to the question, but I stopped him because I wanted to hear what Jim would say.

"Well, if he could get a regular job like other dads, and maybe have an office. I have a friend John, and his brother works with Dad in the car wash. He says everybody working there is younger than Dad. They all make fun of him behind his back."

Pamela was called to testify. She told in detail how much I'd neglected Jim before the divorce.

Our lawyer, in cross-examining her, hammered away at the fact that she was the one who left Jim.

The day ended with Pamela on the stand sobbing, saying how much she missed Jimmy and how much better Whittaker and she could provide for his needs than I could.

We adjourned at five. The judge told us we would reconvene in the morning.

On our way out of the building, our lawyer told us that our judge had a reputation for always giving children to the mother. He asked if I had any knowledge of Pamela committing adultery while we were married. I said no. He said that was too bad, because it would help us if we could prove she'd been stepping out on me before we separated. I angrily told him we didn't need a lawyer with a gutter-mind. He asked if that meant I'd like him to leave the case, and I said yes, and he left.

"Are you sure it was a good idea to do that?" Kellie asked quietly.

"What difference does it make? We've already lost."

We walked outside. The boys were on the lawn throwing a ball.

Suddenly I had a plan to keep my son. "Hey guys, whataya say we take off for Yellowstone National Park now?"

"No kidding?" Jim asked.

"You bet. C'mon, I'll race you both to the car."

They took off. I started to jog after them.

"Michael!" Kellie called out after me.

I stopped.

"You're not planning on running away with Jim, are you?"

"Yes. That's exactly what I'm planning."

"You know that's wrong."

"Since when is it wrong for a father to be with his boy?"

"He's her boy too."

"She doesn't want a boy. She wants a table decoration—somebody to show off when company comes. He wouldn't be happy in Boston."

We all got in the car. I stopped to get gas and some food, and we took off.

Four hours later we were still heading north. The boys were asleep in the backseat.

"You're not very talkative tonight," I said.

"You know how I feel about what you're doing."

"If you don't like it, then why are you going along with me?"

"Because you're my husband."

"Blind obedience?"

"The man I married won't break the law. I'm just waiting for you to come to your senses. Tell me, have you thought about what you're doing? In the eyes of the law, it's kidnapping. Besides, what will you do to keep from getting caught?"

"We'll change our names, and I'll get a job some place."

"I wonder what the judge'll think tomorrow about your little sermon about how much Jesus means in your life when he realizes you've skipped the state."

"What difference does it make what he thinks?"

"Michael, please don't disappoint me. You're one of the few heroes left in my life."

That hurt. "Don't you see?" I said miserably. "If I don't leave with him tonight, they'll take him away from me."

"Even if they do, he'll come back. I know he will."

"Sure," I grumbled, "for two weeks every year."

"No, longer. You're very important to him now. He may not even realize yet how much he needs you. Besides, how much respect for the law is he going to have if you do this? And do you suppose he'll ever join the church if his father is a fugitive from the law?"

I pulled over to the side of the road and grabbed the steering wheel and tried to be a silent rock.

"Maybe if we talked about it," Kellie said.

We could hear the sound of crickets in the summer air. "I wasn't a very good father when he was little, but I really think I've gotten better at it."

She came to me and laid her head on my shoulder. "A boy couldn't have a better dad than you. I really think Rusty's going to turn out all right now. You're a wonderful father."

"If I'm so good at it, then why am I losing Jim?"

"Things'll work out."

"But what if they don't?"

"We'll try and work inside the law." She looked up at me. "Do you want me to drive part way on our way back?"

Slowly I nodded my head. "If you just turn the car around—that'll be the hardest part."

The next day Pamela and Whittaker won custody of Jim.

A week later, they returned to Utah in a rented Cadillac to take my son away from me. I made sure Jim took the tent and sleeping bag and hiking boots I'd bought him the day before. I asked him if he wanted to take any fishing equipment with him, but he said no.

Right after they left, I went in the garage and found his fishing reel and oiled it for him, so it would be ready for him when he came back.

He's not coming back, I thought.

I stayed in the garage for a long time, holding his reel in my hand, remembering our days at Grizzly Gulch.

At one point I looked up and noticed Rusty standing there.

"Can't you see I'm busy?" I said brusquely.

"It's okay if you don't like me anymore," he mumbled.

I set Jim's reel down.

Rusty's head was down. "I'm not as good at things like Jim."

Seconds passed. All I wanted to do was to think about Jim. I remember thinking, Rusty isn't really mine. Let Kellie worry about him.

Then in my mind appeared an image of a blind beggar who had asked Jesus for his eyesight.

Nobody would have minded if Jesus had just walked by. Nobody, that is, except the millions of us, beggars too, who have come along since then. And if a blind beggar is important to God, how about an awkward little boy with bad eyesight?

"Tiger," I said quietly, "come here. I need a hug."

He ran and threw his arms around me.

I gave him my reel, identical to Jim's, and told him that the next time we went fishing, I'd teach him how to cast.

"Saturday?" he asked.

"I promise."

"I'm glad you're my dad," he said.

"Me too," I answered, mussing his hair as we went in the house.

CHAPTER TWELVE

Two months later Pamela phoned from Boston. "Jim's right here next to me," she said, sounding frustrated. "I want you to tell him that all churches are good and that he doesn't have to ride his bicycle ten miles down busy streets to attend a Mormon church when he can go with us to our church. Here he is. Tell him."

"Jim, how's it going?"

"All right."

"Pamela says you're going to a Mormon church there."

"Yeah, it's a long ways away so I have to leave real early."

"Wouldn't you rather just go to church with your mom and Whittaker?"

"I don't like their church."

"Why not?"

"It's too quiet. If you drop a book or something, everybody gets bent out of shape like it was the end of the world. And in their church, after it's over, people just go home. They don't stand around and talk like they do in Provo." He paused. "And they don't have the Book of Mormon. I took one there one time, and this lady saw it and got real mad and told me it was the work of the devil. After that I brought it every time. And I always made sure that lady saw me with it."

I smiled because he was a lot like me.

He continued. "And then I decided I'd better read it, just in case she asked me what was in it." He paused. "It's not too bad, Dad. That's when I started riding my bike to the Mormon church every Sunday."

I asked him to call the bishop and make arrangements for someone in the church to pick him up on their way, so he wouldn't have to ride his bike. It worked out fine.

Two weeks later Jim phoned me. "They won't let me join the church."

"I can't do anything about that," I said.

"Yeah, but I want to join."

"I'm sorry, you'll just have to wait."

"For how long?"

"Until they let you. I'm sorry, but that's the way it is."

In December Pamela phoned me again. "Here's your son. It was bad enough he slept in our backyard all summer, but he can't sleep outside when there's a foot of snow on the ground. He's your son. Talk to him."

"Hi, Jim," I said.

"Hi, Dad."

"Your mom's worried you'll get sick if you camp in the snow."

"The Boy Scout handbook says snow is a good insulator. I've been thinking about building an igloo. What do you think?"

"Look, I really think you'd better sleep in your bedroom until spring comes. I'm just sure your Mom won't feel real comfortable with you out in the snow living in an igloo. I'd say go ahead and build it, and maybe once in a while you can go out there and stay in it, but probably not all night. You gotta realize they're not used to having a mountain man living with them. Okay?"

He was disappointed. "Okay."

Three weeks later she phoned me again. "I just want you to know your son's facing a lawsuit and it's all your fault."

"Why?"

"Some boys in his gym class tried to beat him up. Jim fought back until the teacher stopped the fight. One of the boys has a large bruise on his face where Jim kicked him with his foot. I just got off the phone with the boy's mother. She's talking lawsuit. Now I know you're the one who paid for his karate lessons, so you talk to him. Tell him never to fight again."

"Hi, Jim," I said a minute later.

"Dad, the karate really works."

"I hope you went easy on 'em."

"Yeah, sure. I just wanted to teach them some respect."

"Did it work?"

"I think so. Kids were awfully nice to me afterwards."

For Christmas I sent him a jar of peanuts and a jar of straw-berry jam. I told him to tell his friends that when we spent that summer in the cabin in Montana, we lived on nuts and berries. It was our private joke.

Pamela didn't appreciate mountain-man humor. She told me that over Christmas vacation, since she wouldn't let him sleep in his igloo, he got back at her by setting up a tent in his bedroom and sleeping on the floor every night.

I phoned him on Christmas day. He told me that Whittaker had given him a computer, but the only software he got was called Stock Market Trends.

He asked if I had steady work yet, and I said it looked like I might have a part in a Robert Redford movie in the spring. I was hoping he'd think that Robert Redford and I were just like that.

* * * * *

In March we learned that Kellie was pregnant.

"Don't look so smug," she said with a smile, knowing how proud I was to have her carrying our child.

The New Testament movie was shown on TV the week before Easter. It played two nights during Easter week.

As I realized that people across the country were seeing it, I had a feeling that I had a responsibility to live right.

I decided to repent.

I'd been holding a grudge against Beth since the custody hearings because she'd spoken out against me, but then I got to wondering how she was doing after her divorce. I called her on Good Friday, and we talked, and she told me how tough it had been for her. I offered to send her a little money each month, and although she couldn't bring herself to thank me, she said she wouldn't turn the money down if I sent it.

* * * * *

In April Jim phoned me. "I don't like it here."

"Why not?"

"I tried to talk Whittaker and Mom into having a blessing on the food. Whittaker said people prayed over their food in Bible times, but we didn't need to do that anymore because that's why we have federal meat inspectors." He paused. "Dad, can I come out this summer and stay with you?"

I asked to speak to Pamela. She told me she didn't see how they could work it in, because they were going to Europe for most of the summer. She said that maybe he could come for a few days near the end of August—if, she said with a note of superiority, I could afford the ticket.

*   *   *   *   *

Late one afternoon in June Pamela called from Boston.

"Jimmy is missing. Do you know where he is?"

"I haven't heard from him."

"We were just about to leave on our trip to Europe. Whittaker thought you might've kidnapped him."

"No."

"We dropped him off this morning at his day camp, and when we went back at six to pick him up, they told us he hadn't been there all day."

"Maybe he just played hooky."

"Couldn't he have at least told us?" she asked.

"Pamela, you don't tell your parents when you're going to play hooky. Look, just relax and have supper. He'll be home by dark, so don't worry."

But he didn't come home.

A day passed. Still no word.

I called Whittaker and offered to go out there and help, but he said he doubted if I could do better than the best detective agency in Boston.

That made up my mind. I flew out the next day.

*   *   *   *   *

They lived in a large two-story brick home in Wellesley Hills. I paid for the taxi and took my suitcase up to the front door. I rang the doorbell. It had chimes that played a one-minute melody.

And it took Pamela about that long to walk from her kitchen to the front door. She looked rich and worried.

"Has Jim shown up yet?" I asked.

"No."

"I came to help."

She scowled. "Oh."

"Don't worry, I won't stay here."

"No, that's okay. You'd better. We have plenty of room, and maybe I can give you some ideas of where to look for him."

"Well, okay. Thanks. My funds are a little tight right now."

That was no surprise to her. "Come in."

I followed her inside. There was a dining room off to the left, and large living room to the right, a set of stairs directly in front of the door, and a hallway next to it that led to the other rooms on that floor.

"The guest bedroom is up here."

I followed her upstairs to where I'd be staying. I was pleased with how polite and courteous we both had become.

"I'll put out some guest towels for you."

"Thank you. You're doing very well here, aren't you," I commented.

"We've been very happy."

"I'm glad for you."

"What will you need me to help you with?"

"I'd like to use your telephone, and maybe a list of his friends, school contacts, anything you can think of."

I spent the rest of the afternoon on the phone talking to people on the list Pamela gave me.

Whittaker came home at seven. When he walked in, I was on the phone.

Pamela kissed him hello and then took him to the kitchen for some tomato juice and crackers and an explanation of what I was doing there.

After I finished my call, I went into the kitchen. It was larger than our entire house in Provo.

Whittaker and I shook hands. "You didn't need to come. The detective agency has already made all the contacts you did today."

"Maybe so, but for them it's just a job. With me, it's my son."

"Supper'll be ready in fifteen minutes," Pamela said.

"I can't stay. I'll be leaving in a minute."

"Do you want to use one of our cars?" she asked.

"If I could, that'd be very helpful."

"You do have a valid license, don't you?" Whittaker asked.

"Of course."

"Traffic out here is worse than you're used to in Utah," he said.

"Look, Whittaker, if it's any problem, just forget the car."

"No, no, go right ahead, if that's what Pamela wants."

*   *   *   *   *

Within a day I'd exhausted every possible lead, talked to every teacher, met with every friend. Nobody knew where Jim had gone.

I went into Boston and walked the streets looking for my boy. I had his picture with me, and I'd walk up to people and say, "Excuse me, I'm looking for a lost child. Have you seen anyone that looks like this?"

"No."

A few more feet and then I'd repeat the question.

Day after day I continued. I started in the center of town and worked out. At night I drove back to Pamela's and ate and went to bed.

It was endless, and probably futile. But I had to do something.

Every day I saw thousands of people on the street. Faces in a crowd. Strangers in a hurry. Their sorrow and disappointment and loneliness etched on their faces.

A young teenage girl, trying hard to look a worldly twenty, stood on the corner, watching me come down the street.

"Looking for a good time?" she asked with a strange leer.

I stopped to look at her face. She was chewing gum energetically and avoided looking me in the eye. She wore tight-fitting black pants and a purple shirt buttoned as little as possible. Somehow I knew she was a runaway.

"Your mother cries every time she passes your empty bedroom," I said.

"How do you know?"

"Because my son is missing. This is what he looks like. Have you seen him?"

She looked at the picture and shook her head. "How old is he?"

"Eleven years old."

Her tough-girl expression softened. "I hope you find him."

"Where are you from?" I asked.

She got street-wise again. "It's none of your business."

"You want to know something?"

"What?"

"God loves you," I said.

She unleashed a string of profanity at me.

I moved on.

*   *   *   *   *

I called Kellie every night to see if he'd turned up in Utah. I also phoned Beth and asked her to go out to the cabin and see if he was there. The next day she phoned while I was gone and told Pamela the cabin was empty.

A day later when I came back after searching, Pamela met me at the door. She looked terrible. "The police just called."

"What is it?" I asked, feeling an awful gloom come over me.

"They found a body of a boy about Jim's age. They want someone to go down and see—" she could barely say the words —"if it's Jim."

"I'll go," I said.

She gave a sigh of relief. "I knew I couldn't face it. I'll drive you there."

After a few minutes of silence, she asked, "What will we do if he's dead?"

"I don't know."

"I'm not sure I'd ever get over it," she said.

I nodded. "It'd be very hard."

She pulled in front of the police station. There were no parking places. I told her I'd run in and then meet her there in a few minutes.

A short time later I was walking to the morgue with a police officer.

"How did the boy die?" I asked.

"Stab wounds."

"Who did it?"

"A street gang maybe. We're not sure."

We entered a cold-storage room. He rolled out a metal slab from the wall. A sheet covered the body. "Are you ready?" he asked.

"Yes, go ahead."

He pulled back the sheet. The cold naked body of a boy lay there, his face battered, stab marks in his stomach, a three-inch-long cut across his face. His legs and thighs and lower stomach were black and blue where they'd kicked him over and over again after he'd fallen to the ground.

It wasn't Jim.

I shook my head so the police officer would know it wasn't my son, and then I started gagging. I barely made it to a restroom before I threw up.

A few minutes later, my face drenched in sweat, I walked outside. Pamela's car was double-parked. I got in.

"It wasn't him."

"Thank God."

"Don't thank him too much, Pamela."

"Why not?"

"He was somebody's son."

*   *   *   *   *

The next day I decided I'd done all I could. It was time to return to Utah.

"There's something I want to tell you," Pamela said as she drove me to the airport.

"What?"

"I never had much respect for you before, but now I do. You've become the man I always hoped you'd be."

"Thanks."

At the Salt Lake Airport, when I came into the terminal, Rusty called out my name and ran to hug me. "Dad! Hi! Did you find Jim?"

"No, not yet."

I stood up and hugged Kellie. Being in her arms again made me realize how much I loved her.

We drove back home. Rusty sat next to me, as close as he could.

"Rusty has something to ask you," Kellie said.

"What is it, Tiger?"

"Dad, can I start taking violin lessons again. I like the violin. Is that all right with you? If it isn't, I won't."

I smiled. "I'd be proud to have a violin player in our family. If that's your dream, go for it."

Kellie smiled at him. "I told you that's what he'd say."

The next day I went into the mountains alone and spent the day in fasting and prayer.

That night I woke up suddenly. I'd been dreaming about when Jim and I were at the cabin. I couldn't sleep after that.

I waited until seven in the morning and then called Beth. After hearing her complain about how early it was, I asked her to go out to the cabin again and see if Jim was there.

"Again? I told you before, he's not there. What makes you think he'd be there anyway? He hated it all the time he was there with you."

"Just check it out for me, okay?"

At noon she called back.

"There's nobody there."

"Are you absolutely sure?"

"Look," she said, "I went inside and looked around.

Nobody's living there, I tell you. How many times do I have to drive up there?''

The next night I dreamed again about being at the lake. Was it inspiration or was it nothing? He probably wasn't at the lake, but I had to know for sure.

As soon as it started to get light outside, I got up and dressed. Kellie was still sleeping. I made peanut butter and jelly sandwiches and then went out to the car. I was checking the oil when I looked up and saw Rusty coming outside in his pajamas.

"What are you doing up so early?" he asked.

"I have to go to our cabin in Montana and see if Jim's there." I slammed the hood of the car shut.

"Are you going all by yourself?"

I nodded. "Yeah. Your mom has kids to baby-sit."

"You'd better let me go with you then," he said.

"Why?"

"I can keep you awake so you won't fall asleep while you're driving."

Then it hit me—he'd thought about it before, that if he'd been in the car that fateful night his father would still be alive. And I remembered my dad saying he needed me to help him and how much that meant to me now.

"You're right," I said softly. "I need a partner. Let's go wake your mom and tell her we're going."

*   *   *   *   *

On our first day the water pump in the car went out. After a gas station fixed it, the manager informed me they didn't take checks.

No matter what I said, he wouldn't budge.

"Then keep the car," I muttered angrily, starting out to the road to hitchhike.

Rusty followed after me, doing his best to look as disgusted as I was.

"Hey!" the owner yelled at me.

"What?"

"Is that your kid?"

"Yeah."

He looked at Rusty. "I guess we'll make an exception and take your check."

Early the next afternoon, I turned off the highway onto the dirt road leading to Grizzly Gulch. After what seemed an eternity we came to the lake. I parked the car in front of the cabin.

The door was locked. I found my key and opened it up.

We went inside.

There was nobody there. Suddenly I gave in to the gloom that had hovered around me for days. In my mind I pictured my son being taken and tortured and then slowly killed.

I told Rusty that I wanted to be alone for a while and suggested that he go explore down by the lake. After he left, I looked around the place. There was the same Western paperback I'd read so long ago, and the cot where Dad had stayed the last time. Here is where he'd reached the end of the line, where all his bubbles burst, where he had to give up on lions and the Panama Canal and the miracle cures.

Dad, I miss you so much even now. If you were here, I know you'd help me. We used to fix things, didn't we? A neighbor'd call about a problem and you'd say, Okay, we'll come and take a look at it. And you and me'd go over and fix it. There wasn't anything we couldn't fix, was there. Dad, can you hear me? I need you to help me fix this. I need you to help me find my son. Is he dead? If he's dead, then at least he's with you. Tell him I love him. I don't think I told him enough.

I realized I was sitting on the cot where Jim had slept the summer we were together, and suddenly I hated the cabin and every nail Dad had driven to build it. I had to get away. There were too many memories here.

I stumbled out the door. Rusty was down by the lake skipping rocks across the water. I called for him to come up right away.

"It's nice here," he said as he rounded the top of the trail a minute later. "Are we staying tonight?"

"No, we'll stay with your Aunt Beth. I've decided to sell this old place. It's no good to anyone now. Get in the car. Let's go."

As I turned to get in the car, out of the corner of my eye I saw something move.

"Jim!"

We ran and threw our arms around each other. Rusty joined in, and the three of us hugged and cried.

We returned to the cabin, and he told us how he'd saved the allowance money Whittaker gave him until he had enough for a bus ticket to Montana. The first time Beth came to look for him, he was in the cabin at the time, but she didn't go inside. She just looked in from the window. Jim was just inside the door. After that, he got up each morning and took everything that looked like someone was staying there and hid them in the woods, and each night he crept back. Because of that, the second time she came, she didn't suspect anything.

Jim was thinner than I'd ever seen him. I asked him what he'd been eating while he'd been here, and he grinned and said nuts and berries.

"But why did you come here?" I asked.

"What I really wanted was to go stay with you in Utah, but I knew you'd call Mom and she'd make you send me back again. So I came here."

"But you hated it before, didn't you?"

"I know." He paused as if he wasn't sure if he dare say it. "But this place reminds me of you, Dad. That's why I came, because it was the closest I could get to you."

I knew what he meant.

We drove to the store by the lake and phoned Pamela, but there was no answer. I bought us lunch. I'd never seen a boy eat so much.

After we'd finished eating, I phoned again. Still no answer. We decided to go fishing. Jim's bobber dropped below the surface, and he set the hook. A large trout cleared the water.

"All right! What a whale!" I shouted.

Jim reeled, but the fish continued to pull line off the reel.

"Don't let him get to those logs!" I cautioned.

Jim moved up the lakeshore to get away from the sunken timber.

I ran to the cabin for the big net. By the time I got back, Jim had the fish nearly to the shore. I dipped the net into the water and lifted it out.

"Look at this, everybody!" I yelled, proudly showing it off to the fishermen on the lake. "My son caught this!"

We drove back to the general store. "Dad, do we have to tell Mom right away?"

"Yeah, we do. She's really been worried about you."

At the store Jim and Rusty sat on the dock while I phoned Pamela on the outdoor pay phone. This time she answered.

I told her all about Jim. "I don't understand that at all," she said. "If he wanted to go to camp, why didn't he just tell us? After all Whittaker and I've done for him, and this is the way he treats us."

I didn't want to delay what I knew had to be done. "How do you want me to send him back to you, air freight or parcel post?"

"Just a minute. Let me have you talk to Whittaker."

Whittaker came on the line. "Thanks for finding the boy. Pamela says he's at a lake. Do they have structured camp activities there? If they do, maybe he could stay there for the summer. I mean, if that's what he wants. We just want him to have whatever he wants. The only thing is, we're never sure what he wants. He's a very difficult boy, you know. He would've slept in the snow all winter if we'd let him. There's no figuring him out."

"Whittaker, I'd be willing to take him off your hands."

He paused. "For how long?"

"Forever."

"You're saying you'd like to get back custody of the boy?"

"That's right."

"Hang on."

There was a long silence. Then Pamela said, "Let me talk to Jimmy."

I yelled for Jim. "Mom wants to talk to you."

He came up from the lake and I handed him the phone. "Hi, Mom."

A long silence at our end. "I'm sorry you worried so much

. . . I don't like it in Boston . . . I don't want to go to Europe . . . I like it out here . . . I don't care if he is poor, he's still my dad . . . All right, I love you too . . .''

He handed back the phone and went down to the dock to be with Rusty.

Pamela was crying. "It was so much easier when he was little," she sobbed.

"I know."

"And if you hadn't completely warped his mind when he was with you, it'd be a whole lot easier for Whittaker and me to handle him now."

"You're probably right."

"And now he's about to enter puberty," she said. "Who knows what he'll be like then?"

"You're right. It could be trouble no matter who has him."

She paused. "I guess it'd be okay if you take custody, provided you'll let him come visit us a few times a year."

"Pamela, don't talk about this unless you're serious. I don't think I could stand to lose him twice."

She sighed. "Well, it's what Jim wants, so I guess that's what we should do. I'll have our lawyer draw up the papers."

"Pamela, you know what this means to me. All I can say is thanks. I promise to take good care of our boy."

"I know you will, Michael. You've changed a lot lately. I'm curious though. What's made the difference?"

I thought about Jesus and my dad and Kellie and even Steve. "I've had good examples to follow."

We said our goodbyes and hung up.

Jim and Rusty were standing on the dock. I ran toward them, yelling *Geronimo!* at the top of my voice. When I got to the edge of the dock, I grabbed one in each arm and jumped off the dock.

The three of us sailed through the air.

And landed with a splash in the cold water of our mountain lake.

We were home at last.